Level Zero
The Pact of Zeros
Raymond Riddle "Panda of Pandemonium"

Panda's Prints

Copyright © 2025 by Raymond Riddle "The Panda of Pandemonium"

All rights reserved.

No portion of this book may be reproduced in any form without written permission from the publisher or author, except as permitted by U.S. copyright law.

Contents

Chapter 1
Jax

Jax Renner gripped his wooden stick like a hero about to slay a dragon. He stood near the gate to the chicken pen, chest swelling in response to the imagined roaring of an arena crowd. In his mind, there were banners with his name stitched in gold, whole guilds chanting for him, noble girls swooning. He swung the stick once, twice, the satisfying whoosh it made through the air.

The reality? A half-asleep chicken blinked at him, unimpressed.

"Prepare yourself, foul beast!" Jax declared, jabbing the stick in the air.

The chicken flapped its wings and darted to the side. Jax stumbled after it, tripped on the straw, and almost fell face-first into the feed trough. The other chickens scattered in a panicked flurry of clucks and feathers, one of them pecking at his leg as it fled. Jax yelped, hopping on one foot, swinging his "sword" in the air like he was fending off invisible demons.

From the fence came a chorus of laughter. Three kids leaned against the wooden posts, enjoying the show.

"Look at him! Training to fight monsters with chickens!"

"Careful, Level Zero," another teased, tapping the glowing Band on his wrist. The number shimmered at Level 3, as if mocking Jax.

"Maybe beat a bird before you dream about guild trials."

Jax straightened, face red, gripping his stick tighter. His own Band sat on his wrist, dull and lifeless. Not a flicker, not a glow. It had been that way since he was born. Sixteen years, and still nothing. Level Zero.

He hated the way it sounded. Like he was nothing at all.

"Laugh all you want," Jax shouted back, forcing himself to remain calm. "One day, you'll be the ones lining up to watch me in the Arena!"

The kids rolled their eyes, laughing under their breath as they walked away. Their glowing Bands caught the sunlight, and Jax's cheeks burned hotter than the straw scattered around him.

He turned back to the chickens, raising his stick again.

"Fine. They don't believe in me? I'll make them believe."

He charged into the pen once more, swinging with everything he had. The chickens scattered again. One flapped straight into his face, wings beating frantically, and Jax stumbled backward, tripping over the feed bucket.

For a moment, he just lay there, staring at the pale blue sky.

"I'm not nothing," he whispered, only the chickens hearing him.

"I'll prove it. Somehow."

A few minutes later, Jax stomped out of the chicken pen with feathers stuck in his hair. He swung his stick-sword over his shoulder like he'd just returned from a glorious battle, even though his face was flushed and his tunic was smeared with dirt.

"Victory!" he shouted to no one in particular. "The beasts are defeated!"

Old Marna, the baker's wife, was passing by with a basket of rolls. She stopped, lips twitching as she tried not to laugh.

"Did the chickens surrender this time, Jax?"

"They never stood a chance," Jax said, puffing out his chest.

Marna chuckled and tossed him a roll.

"Keep practicing, dear. You've got the spirit."

Jax bit into the roll like it was a reward for valor, ignoring the way she talked to herself as she walked away: "Poor boy. Still no glow on that Band..."

It was always like that.

The adults in the village liked him well enough. He was loud, stubborn, funny. Always charging into something with that wild grin, even when he had no hope of winning. Kids rolled their eyes at him, but the adults? They smiled at his enthusiasm, before turning away with pity in their eyes.

Level Zero. That was what they saw, no matter how hard he swung his stick or shouted his dreams.

"Don't worry, Jax," his father had said just last night while patching a hole in his boots. "Some children take longer to awaken. Your time will come."

His mother had nodded, her smile warm but thin. "Yes, love. Sometimes it takes a little more to jumpstart the flames."

They meant well, but Jax could hear what they didn't say: *Maybe it'll never come.*

He clenched his fists now, glaring at his dull Band. "I'll make it come," he growled. "I don't care if I have to fight every monster in the woods with a stick. I'm not staying Zero forever."

The chickens clucked nervously, as if they sensed his temper boiling again. Jax jabbed his stick at the ground like he was stabbing the thought itself.

"GRR!" he shouted, loud enough to startle a cat off a fence.

The cat hissed, sprinted away, and Jax spun toward it. "Hey, come back! I'll fight you too if I have to!"

Marching away from the barnyard he heard the villagers chuckling as they went about their work. They were kind chuckles, the sort people gave a child still pretending. He clenched his jaw. *They don't get it. I'm not pretending. I'm training.*

That was when he overheard it.

Two hunters walked past, bows over their backs, speaking in low voices.

"...herd's been sighted near the river bend. Three days, maybe less, before we've got the equipment ready for the hunt, but they're close enough to start scouting."

Jax froze, heart pounding. *A Rampiro herd.*

The great horned beasts were massive, elegant and brawny, their antlers curled into angles that could sheer a tree in half. Harmless enough if left alone, but if they stampeded? A forest could become a fueld of felled timber in seconds. Every season, the hunters culled a few. The village feasted, and young hunters, the assistants, got their first real XP.

The Rampiro hunt was the closest thing Hreli had to a festival. For some, it was the day they finally became Level Ones.

Jax's grip tightened on his stick.

"Three days," he whispered. *That was too long.* By then, the hunters would swoop in, the other kids in tow, and he'd be shoved to the back. Maybe he'd get a measly 10 XP as an "assistant." Enough for scraps. Enough for pity.

But not for glory.

He looked down at his Band's inactive state. He imagined the Rampiro's antlers reflecting the moonlight, imagined himself landing a killing blow, his Band flaring alive for the first time — not with scraps, but with a full 100 XP. Enough to burst into Level One in one glorious moment.

"They'll never call me Zero again," he muttered.

The forest beyond the fields loomed heavy with shadows deepening between the trees. That was where the Rampiro grazed. That was where the hunters would go in three days. He had to get there first.

Jax's mouth twisted into that wild grin that made adults sigh and mutter "reckless boy" under their breath.

"Sangabi didn't wait for permission," he said to himself. "Neither will I."

And with a stick for a sword and fire in his veins, Jax marched straight toward the tree line, chasing a herd that could trample him flat...or make him a hero.

Chapter 2
Tovi

Tovi Amsel's room looked less like a bedroom and more like a paper storm had swallowed it whole. Pages scrawled with numbers littered his desk, his floor, even the top of his bed. Charts ran up the walls like climbing ivy, drawn in cramped handwriting: equations, ratios, arrows pointing to boxes labeled XP gain? and Band resonance??

He squinted at the latest sheet, tapping the back of his charcoal pencil against the side of his nose. The contents though written by him, baffled his mind.

Band Mechanics (v6.3)

1. Base Rule — Contribution: A Band glows when you directly contribute to an outcome (injure, restrain, heal, discover). Magnitude = proportional to contribution.

2. Assists — Fractional Yield: Non-decisive help yields smaller pulses ("assist ticks"). Trackable if repeated.

3. Resonance Events: Certain aligned inputs (materials, intent, mass emotion) can amplify pulses. Hypothesis: menth compounds and synchronized crowds modulate Bands without standard 'kill' inputs.

Tests (next available day):

A. Menth-Field: Control distance, dose, and wind. Observe Band micro-pulse vs. baseline. Repeat thrice; average.

B. Crowd-Chant: Record Band shimmer before/after a unified chant in an arena section. Confirm latency and decay curve. (If positive, explore intent alignment.)

Open Questions:

• Does caregiving (non-combat) ever count as "contribution"?

• Are pulses tied to intent or outcome?

• Do certain guild rites bake in resonance on purpose?

"Hmm...Eighty-five if shared evenly, one-twenty if assisted, but if killshot doubles then—"

The charcoal snapped in his hand.

Tovi scowled, brushing the crumbs aside. None of his calculations worked. The numbers slipped away like sand through his fingers.

From downstairs came his mother's voice: "Tovi! Lanterns in ten minutes!"

"I'll be there," he called back, though his eyes were still locked on the Band circling his wrist. It glowed blue, a soft halo of light marking him at Level 0. A pathetic flicker, compared to the golden shine of the other apprentices in town.

He pressed the Band against the paper, as if it might leave behind a secret mark. There had to be a pattern. Sangabi didn't just swing her sword. Liora Diorble, The Skeletal Envoy of Light, figured out how to weave tactics into the fight itself. She proved XP can be... bent.

The name always lit a fire in him. Liora, the legendary scholar-warrior, who could solve a battlefield like it was a puzzle box. Tovi wanted to be her more than anything.

"Maybe," he muttered, voice lowering as though the papers might overhear, "maybe XP can be hacked."

He tried a new angle: Band glow compared to distance, hits compared to assists, environmental factors... If he could just pin it down, he could force his way up faster. Not wait for luck or pity hunts. Not scrape up XP crumbs.

A bang outside jolted him from his thoughts. Someone was probably still shouting about Rampiro sightings near the forest edge; half the village had been buzzing since morning. Tovi rolled his eyes.

"Rampiro this, Rampiro that. Let the hunters swing their spears. I'll be the one who rewrites the system."

He didn't notice the faint flicker his Band gave at the words, like it was listening.

The aroma of roasted Gornian meat still clung to the streets of Wihflan, even days after the hunt. Kids strutted with greasy fingers, their Bands flashing brighter than they had a week ago. Every conversation seemed to circle back to who had gotten the best strike, who had landed the kill, who had eaten the richest cut.

Tovi had overheard three boys near the well just this morning, boasting.

"My Band ticked twenty-five from the assist." "Ha! Mine shot up fifty when I speared it in the haunch!" "Yeah, but Bryn hit a hundred. Straight to Level One in a single strike."

They had laughed together, knocking their glowing Bands against each other like mugs of cider.

Tovi had slipped past quietly. His own Band still glowed faint blue, hovering close to Level 1 but not there. He hadn't joined the hunt. Not because he couldn't, but because he hadn't wanted to waste the moment.

While they had shouted and swung spears, he had sat on the ridge, charcoal scratching across the page. Every movement of the Gornians had been noted: speed, patterns, how they circled, how they chose their prey. The strangest detail wasn't in the pack at all.

A full-grown Gornian broke stride mid-lunge. One instant its teeth were bared at an apprentice, the next its legs wobbled and it staggered, claws gouging dirt. It had coughed like smoke was in its throat, tail lashing in panic.

The hunters hadn't noticed, too busy shouting and loosing arrows. Tovi's gaze had caught the patch of menth-leaf crushed beneath the beast's claws. The sharp, bitter herb grew wild near the riverbank, ignored by everyone except apothecaries. The Gornian had faltered right there, wheezing like the scent itself had knocked it off balance.

Tovi had plucked a sprig after the hunt, pressing it into his notebook.

Now it lay in his hand as he sat at his cluttered desk, dried edges curling but still carrying that sharp tang. He crushed it between his fingers, inhaled the bitter scent. His Band flickered at the same moment. Not a number change—just a pulse.

"Why did you falter?" he whispered to the dried leaf, remembering the beast's sudden stumble. "You were in the middle of attacking. There was no fear, no pain. Was it this?"

He scribbled in his journal, scrawling until the lines thinned the page: Subject recoiled before arrow impact. Breathing labored. Eyes watering. No blade contact. Menth-leaf = possible trigger.

The Band pulsed again, faint and fleeting. He pressed his wrist to the page as if to force it to respond. Nothing. Just the faint glow of almost-Level-One mocking him.

He leaned back, staring up at the ceiling covered in his scribbled charts.

The other kids were basking in their new strength. They had leveled the way everyone always had: blades, blood, meat. But what if they were all blind? What if XP wasn't only about killing? What if choices, environments, understanding played a greater role?

"Sangabi had her blade," he uttered under his breath. "Diestel had his brute force. But Liora Diorble... she bent the rules. She proved the system could be hacked."

His voice dropped lower, almost conspiratorial.

"What if she wasn't the only one?"

The Band gave one more tiny flicker, like it approved.

Tovi stared at it, then at the sprig of menth-leaf, and finally at the mess of papers around him.

He was close. He could feel it. If he could test this theory, prove it, maybe he wouldn't just scrape into Level One—maybe he'd leap past it. Not by stabbing a beast, but by outsmarting the system itself.

Tovi smiled.

His first test was, frankly, pathetic.

He crouched in the back garden with a cage borrowed from the chicken coop, menth-leaf crumbled in his hands. The unfortunate subject: a fat, twitchy-nosed field mouse he'd baited with crumbs.

He pushed the crushed leaf through the bars. The mouse sniffed it, sneezed, and then ate the whole thing.

Tovi groaned documenting his find.

Test #1 — subject unaffected. Conclusion: non-hostile creatures = immune? Or I'm a fool.

The Band didn't so much as twitch.

He tried again with a few garden lizards; same result. One scurried off with the leaf dangling from its mouth like a trophy.

Tovi slumped against the wall.

"So it only works on Gornians... if it works at all? Perfect. Just perfect."

Memories of the beast staggering wouldn't leave him. The way it had gasped, claws dragging, before the spear ever touched it. That had been real. He was sure of it.

His charcoal scratched again.

Test #2 — hypothesis: Gornian-exclusive sensitivity. Must confirm with live subjects.

He looked towards the treeline of the forest.

It was foolish. Gornians were pack hunters. Even a lone one could gut him in seconds. But his theory gnawed at him like a hunger. If he was right, if menth-leaf could stagger them, it was more than science—it was a weapon. A new path to XP. Maybe even to breaking the system.

"Sangabi charged dragons," he muttered, stuffing dried sprigs into his bag. "I can handle a lizard with feathers."

He paused at his door, his mother's voice floating from inside the house.

"Tovi? Lanterns soon. Don't stay out too late."

He hesitated. He could turn back. He could keep studying notes, keep pretending he wasn't slipping behind while every other kid wore their new levels like medals.

Instead, he pulled the strap of the satchel tighter and stepped into the twilight.

The forest loomed ahead, branches shifting like the jaws of a waiting beast. Somewhere in those shadows, a Gornian pack roamed. Tovi's pulse hammered in his ears, but he couldn't stop smiling.

Because if he was right, he wouldn't just catch up. He'd change everything.

Chapter 3
Jax

The forest loomed like a wall of green fire as Jax stood at its edge; a wooden staff balanced across his shoulders, a nervous twitch to his lips. His Band was still dull, his boots already muddy, but tonight...tonight...would change everything.

"Rampiro," he whispered like it was a prayer.

Every hunter in Hreli said the same thing: Never go in alone. Rampiro are docile until they're not. One wrong move, and the herd will crush you flat.

Jax wasn't planning on getting crushed. He was planning on glory. The Wihflan brats could strut about with their flashy Bands from killing Gornians, then he, Jax Renner, would level even higher by taking down a Rampiro first. Before the hunters. Before anyone else.

He stepped under the trees, shadows curling around him.

The ground was soft with moss, shafts of silver moonlight cutting between the branches. He crouched low, the way he'd seen the hunters do, and whispered, "Quiet as a shadow. Quick as a fox." Then he snapped a branch underfoot.

A flock of sparrows exploded out of the trees, wings beating like drums. Jax flinched, heart hammering.

He forced himself to laugh it off.

"Just testing my reflexes."

He pushed deeper, trying to imitate the hunters' crouch-walk. His stick kept getting tangled in vines and his boots squelched in a mud patch. At one point, he almost tumbled headfirst into a burrow. By the time he stopped to catch his breath, sweat was trickling down his back. There had been no change to his Band.

"Fine," he whispered. "They don't give XP for sneaking. I'll just find the herd and earn it."

He knelt, examining the dirt for signs of hooves. Hunters always said to look for tracks. But all he saw was... well, a lot of dirt. And maybe a rabbit print. Or was that a squirrel?

"Tracks," he declared. "Definitely Rampiro. Big herd. Close by."

Somewhere in the distance, the forest gave a low, unsettling rumble. Jax froze, grin faltering.

"Rampiro?" he whispered.

Deep down, the sound hadn't felt like hooves at all.

Pressing deeper into the trees, each step was louder than he wanted. The rumble had faded now, swallowed by the night, but in his chest it still shook like a heartbeat.

"That was Rampiro," he told himself, gripping his stick like it was a lance. "Has to be. Big herd. I'll get one before the hunters even string their bows."

He crouched low, trying to do what he'd seen the hunters do, eyes on the ground, scanning for signs. But all he found were trampled weeds and a lump of moss. Still, he stabbed at it with the stick.

"Tracks," he declared, squatting in imitation, a hand on his chin. "Definitely Rampiro. Probably six. No—ten!" He straightened proudly, as though he'd cracked some great code.

In truth, his stomach fluttered. Real hunters could tell the difference between a rabbit trail and a herd's path. Real hunters had Bands that glowed, proof they belonged out here. His was still dull and lifeless.

But he shoved the doubt down.

"Doesn't matter. Wihflan kids are already bragging about their Gornians. Hreli can't fall behind. And I sure won't." He forward, as if sheer confidence could make the forest bend to him.

Branches clawed at his arms. Twigs snapped underfoot. Somewhere above, an owl hooted, low and mournful. Then came another sound. A chittering that made the hairs on his neck rise. Not the heavy bellows of Rampiro. This was smoother, more sinister.

He froze, straining his ears, as nearby leaves rustled. He thought something darted between the shadows. It was too fast to see clearly. Worry caused his grip on the stick to tighten.

"Alright," he whispered. "Not Rampiro. But maybe... deer? Or foxes?"

The sound came again, the distinct stripping of bark from trees. It was in front of him, then another from the right, then two more from the left. His mouth went dry, forcing a shaken grin.

"Heh. Just the forest playing tricks. Even Sangabi Emcor had to start somewhere, right?" He jabbed the air with his stick, trying to look fierce. "Jax the Brave doesn't scare easily!"

The brush shifted ahead. Two eyes gleamed at him, bright and cruel. Then four. Six. A dozen.

Shapes slinked from the dark; narrow, lean bodies built for speed, tails twitching like whips. Their teeth caught the moonlight.

Gornians.

Jax's blood went cold. He'd heard stories. Pack hunters, smart enough to circle their prey. Kids from Wihflan wore their scars with pride. Even grown hunters never faced them alone.

And here he stood, in the dark, with nothing but a stick.

His grin cracked, but he forced it back. "Well," he croaked, "guess I'll just... level faster than planned."

The Gornians continued slinking from the brush like shadows peeling away from the trees. Their scales rippled under the moonlight. Their claws clicked against roots as they spread out, circling. One flicked its tongue, a snake-quick lash that caught the scent of him.

Jax lifted his stick, forcing his knees to lock even though every part of him screamed to run. "Come on then!" His voice rang higher than he wanted, but he tried to solidify his stance. "You think I'm scared? Jax the Brave doesn't run from lizards!"

The beasts answered with a low hiss, glazing at each other, tails twitching in eerie rhythm.

One lunged, faster than his eye could follow. Jax swung down with all his might, the stick cracking through the air. The satisfying thud of impact was followed by the hollow snap of wood splitting clean in two.

The Gornian flinched. Its head whipped, jaws clamping onto the splintered end, yanking it free of his grip. Jax stumbled backward, looking between them and his now empty hands.

The pack shifted closer, a dozen glowing eyes blinking from the dark. Their bodies moved in sync, circling like the hunters' dogs back home, only hungrier.

"Fine!" Jax barked, voice shaky now. "Didn't need that anyway!" His hand shot to his belt where the small leather sheath rested. He tore free the knife his father had given him two summers past. The handle was worn smooth from being turned over in nervous hands.

He could still feel his father's quiet voice when he'd pressed it into Jax's palm: Only when you must. Promise me.

"Well, Dad," Jax murmured through his teeth, raising the blade, "I must."

The next Gornian darted in, jaws wide. Jax slashed. The blade screeched across its scaled hide, leaving only a shallow cut. The beast shrieked, eyes blazing, and swiped with its claws.

Agony enveloped Jax, three lines now torn from shoulder to elbow. He screamed, half in rage, half in terror. Blood trickled down, hot and sticky.

"Ha!" he forced out, his grin wild and crooked. "So you bleed too! Not so tough now, are you?"

Another slammed into his side before he could finish, a heavy weight knocking him flat on his back; the knife skittering through the underbrush, vanishing into the dark. Rolling to his feet, claws raked furrows in the ground beside where his ribs once were, as the Gornian snapped inches from his throat. Its breath reeked of iron and rot, hot against his face.

Jax twisted, kicking with both legs. His boot connected with its snout, buying him a second, the creature snarling and sniffing at the sudden jolt of pain. He scrambled, hand groping through leaves until his fingers brushed the knife. Jax clutched it, rolled, and jabbed upward. The blade scraped under the beast's jaw.

It shrieked and leapt back, vanishing into the circling pack.

Jax staggered to his feet, panting hard. His arm burned, his knees shook, but his smirk returned, defiant and desperate. "You see that? Jax Renner! Took you down with a—"

Another shadow leapt from his blind side, claws raking across the back of his shoulders. He stumbled forward, gasping, knife slipping in his sweaty grip. The hiss of the pack rose around him, louder now, pressing in from every side.

They were toying with him. Testing him.

Birds burst from the trees above, shrieking into the night. Jax's breath hitched. His father's knife trembled in his hand. His Band, dull and lifeless, gave not even a flicker.

This wasn't glory. This wasn't Sangabi splitting the sky or Diestel standing unbroken in the Arena. This was Jax Renner, a boy with nothing but a too small blade and shaky confidence, standing in the middle of a pack of predators that could tear him apart in seconds.

The bravado cracked, mouth going dry.

"...oh sparks."

The Gornians lunged, and Jax's knife flashed in a frantic arc. Metal scraped against claws, sparks spitting in the dark. One beast shrieked as the blade nicked its snout, but the rest pressed closer, jaws snapping.

Jax slashed, stumbled, kicked—then a claw raked across his calf. He yelped, tumbling into the dirt, and his knife almost slipped from his hand again.

They swarmed. Claws gouged the ground around him, teeth clashing inches from his arm; the pack's hissing growing louder with each moment

"Okay—okay, bad idea!" Jax barked, scrambling upright. His bravado, once a fire in his chest, cracked and guttered. His eyes darted between the glowing pairs of eyes closing in.

I'm not Sangabi. I'm not Diestel. I'm just—

One lunged. He dove aside, rolling through brambles. Thorns tore his shirt. Another lunged from the left. He swung his arm and felt claws rip a line across his shoulder. His body screamed with torment.

And then his legs moved before his brain decided.

He ran.

Branches whipped his face. Roots clawed at his boots. His heart pounded so loud he thought the beasts would hear him. Behind him, the Gornians surged like a tide, claws clattering against bark, shrieks rattling the air.

Every snap of teeth was closer. Every hiss curled down his spine.

"Not—like—this!" he panted between breaths. "Jax Renner...doesn't die...at Level Zero!"

The forest itself seemed to join the chase. Birds burst into the air. Rabbits streaked across his path. Leaves trembled as though the trees themselves leaned away from the oncoming pack.

A heavy crash thundered somewhere to his right. Trees shook, and the ground shivered beneath his boots. The sound was deeper than the Gornians, heavier, rolling like thunder.

Jax's eyes widened even as he sprinted. Rampiro.

For a second his spirits rose.

If I can get them into the herd—if the Rampiro trample them—I win! I level! I—

Another Gornian's jaws snapped an inch from his elbow, causing him to veer right sharply, lungs burning. His knife was still in his hand somehow, but his grip was slippery with sweat.

The crash came again, louder. Branches splintered, a tree splitting with a thunderous crack. Something enormous was moving through the dark; shoving everything aside in its panic.

Jax realized, too late, what it meant.

The Gornians weren't just chasing him. They were driving him. Herding him the way wolves did with deer. Straight into the path of the stampeding Rampiro.

Jax ran blind through the noise and motion. His arms burned from claw slashes, and his father's knife shook in his grip. The Gornians shrieked behind him, snapping jaws so close he could feel the heat of their breath. Their claws raked bark as they leapt from trunk to trunk, driving him closer to the sound of the herd.

But it wasn't just him they were herding.

The thunder of hooves grew deafening. The ground buckled under their weight. Branches snapped like kindling. Through gaps in the brush, Jax glimpsed them...the Rampiro herd.

They were colossal, horns like twisted trees, shoulders taller than he was. Their eyes rolled white with terror, mouths bellowing in deep, resonant cries that rattled the air. Steam poured from their nostrils as they plowed through the forest, muscles rippling under shaggy coats.

And the Gornians were everywhere, darting at their flanks, snapping at calves' legs, leaping for throats but darting away at the last second. They weren't killing yet. They were pushing. Driving them straight toward Jax.

His stomach dropped.

"Great," he wheezed. "Gornians behind me, Rampiro on my right. Hero's life, Jax! Hero life."

At that moment a tree exploded behind him, Rampiro antlers shearing the trunk in half. Splinters whistled through the air, one nicking his cheek. Jax stumbled, then forced himself forward again. Chest aching while panic shoved his legs faster than he thought possible.

The forest narrowed suddenly, funneling into a stretch where roots rose like knotted walls. Jax vaulted one, scraped his shin on another, and kept going. The Gornians poured after him, claws scrabbling, tails slicing the air. One snapped at his boot hoping to take out his heel.

Jax screamed and swung the knife backward. The blade met flesh with a hiss. The beast yelped and pulled back, but another immediately filled its place.

The ground shook harder. Louder. The Rampiro were almost on top of him now. He risked a glance and saw antlers crashing through the trees like a tidal wave of bone and muscle. The herd was going to plow right through him.

And then, out of nowhere, something slammed into his side.

Jax staggered, knife jerking in his grip. Another boy had barreled out of the trees, smaller than him, face pale in the moonlight, a satchel clutched against his chest.

"Hey!" Jax shouted, breathless. "Watch it!"

"You watch it!" the boy snapped back, glasses crooked, eyes wild. His voice waffled with the same panic Jax felt pounding beneath his own ribs.

Staring in disbelief at their interaction, didn't slow their speed. The forest roared all around them, their hearts iced over in response. Rampiro bellows echoed so close they rattled Jax's bones. A shadow fell over them, and he barely had time to shove the boy before antlers as wide as a gate swept through the air. The beast barreled past, hooves pounding craters in the dirt. The ground heaved, throwing Jax aside.

"Are you trying to get us killed?!" the boy shouted, scrambling upright.

"I was trying to save you, moron! I was doing fine until you showed up!" Jax snapped back, though his voice cracked mid-yell.

No time for more. The Gornians surged, thrilled by the doubled prey. One lunged for the new kid. Jax, without thinking, slashed with his knife, cutting across its muzzle. The beast shrieked and twisted away.

Another came for Jax from behind, but the boy shoved him forward, knocking him clear as claws scraped the dirt where his back had been.

The Rampiro screamed, surging faster, trampling bushes and small trees. The Gornians wove between their legs, snapping at calves, darting at the boys whenever they lagged. The entire herd had been whipped into a frenzy, with the introduction of the Gornians; driving forward in blind terror.

"Run!" the boy yelled.

"I am running!" Jax shouted back, leaping a fell tree trunk.

Side by side they bolted, weaving between trees, ducking antlers, dodging snapping jaws. Their breaths came ragged, their feet pounded in rhythm, their Bands, dull though they were, seemed to throb in the same terrified beat.

The forest strobe-flashed with moonlight and shadow. Trees toppled, dirt sprayed, leaves rained from above. The noise was unbearable: Rampiro bellows, Gornians shrieks, branches snapping, hooves like thunder.

For a moment, Jax thought he saw Sangabi herself in the chaos, her legend blazing in his mind, the kind of fight she would have carved into glory. But the pain raging across his body from the Gornian's earlier attacks, brought him back to reality, crushing the thought.

He wasn't Sangabi. He wasn't a hero. He was Jax Renner, Level Zero, running for his life with some stranger who was just as doomed.

Yet when he risked a glance at the boy, saw the same fear blazing in his eyes; Jax felt something besides fear flicker inside himself.

Chapter 4
Tovi

The forest was colder than Tovi expected. Dew clung to the undergrowth, soaking the hem of his tunic as he pushed through the brush. His satchel bumped against his side with every step, the bundle of dried menth-leaf sprigs rattling inside.

He had told himself he'd only come for a short test. A glance at the Gornians, a cautious sprinkle of the leaf, nothing foolish. But every step deeper made his pulse quicken with a strange mix of dread and exhilaration.

He adjusted his glasses, repeating his findings under his breath.

"Test three: live subject. Hypothesis: Gornian-exclusive sensitivity to menth. Sub-hypothesis: possible XP effect without combat. Notes to follow."

It sounded brave when he said it aloud. Almost like Liora Diorble herself might have once uttered while adding entries into her Codex, The Mandates of Living Death, bent over her experiments.

But his hands were trembling.

The forest air grew heavier the deeper Tovi pushed in. His pack strap dug into his shoulder, the menth-leaf sprigs inside their jars rattling like dry bones with every step. The cold dew soaked his boots, and he shivered, though not from the chill. His notebook was already half-filled with sketches and half-baked formulas, and tonight, he was determined to test them.

Gornians. That was the plan. A single specimen was all he needed. Observe its reaction to the menth, record the results, prove his hypothesis: XP could be drawn from interactions, not just combat.

He crouched near a clearing, sprinkling crumbled menth on the dirt. The sharp, bitter scent stung his nose.

He waited. Minutes passed. Nothing but the rustle of branches.

Then a shadow shifted near the treeline. Tovi froze, heart hammering. Sleek, long, and low to the ground. A Gornian? His pulse quickened.

He fumbled for his notebook, then the shadow rose. Higher. Much higher.

Tovi's breath caught in his throat. That wasn't a Gornian.

Through the brush, the massive, hulking head of a furred beast lifted. What he had thought was the slinky body of the reptilian Gornian had, in fact, been the bulk of a male Rampiro's antlers. Spread wide, it glinted like twisted bronze against the piercing light of the moon. Its nostrils flared, drawing in the bitter menth, and its eyes rolled white with agitation.

"Oh no," Tovi whispered.

The Rampiro snorted, pawing the ground. Branches shook as its bulk pressed forward, muscles coiling tight. Then it bellowed, the sound was so deep it rattled Tovi's bones, then it charged.

The ground shook beneath his feet.

Tovi staggered back, yanking his satchel clear of branches, his notes spilling loose.

"Not you—! I wasn't after you—!"

But the bull didn't care. It barreled past him, tearing up earth with its hooves, crashing through the undergrowth with unstoppable force.

And it wasn't alone.

From deeper in the woods, other Rampiro bellowed, the herd answering the bull's panic. The thunder of hooves rose like a storm, trees bowing as massive bodies plowed through the forest.

The herd was stampeding.

Tovi's knees buckled. He had seen Rampiro from afar, docile and slow-grazing, their antlers tangled with morning mist. But this, this was a wall of muscle and horn and terror. Each bellow was a death knell.

He bolted.

Branches whipped his face, but he didn't dare stop. His glasses slid down his nose, his breath struggling to escape his lungs. Behind him, the Rampiro screamed, crashing through trees like bladed battering rams culling the vegetation in their path.

The menth-leaf had ruined everything. He hadn't repelled Gornians, he'd agitated the largest beasts in the valley.

And then, through the chaos, another figure.

A boy, charging through the trees from the opposite side, knife flashing in his fist, hair wild, face smeared with dirt and blood. He was running the same way, just as hunted, Gornians snapping at his heels.

Tovi panicked, the boy's shoulder smashing into his.

They collided, stumbling a few strides. His glasses flew from his face, notes scattered into the air. He clawed for them, only to be shoved aside as antlers crashed through the space he'd fallen.

"Hey, watch it!" the boy shouted.

"You, watch it!" Tovi snapped back, fumbling his glasses onto his nose.

No time for blame or explanations.

Only one choice: run.

The roaring bellows began sounding different. They weren't the sound of Rampiro. This was a higher, sharper sound, chittering shrieks that sliced through the night air.

Tovi's blood ran cold.

Gornians.

They must have been with the other boy was running from. The predators slipped into the frenzy like knives through silk. He glimpsed them weaving between the Rampiro legs, snapping at flanks, darting at calves. Their tails cracked like whips, their claws scraped sparks from stone.

The herd bellowed louder, more frantic, surging faster.

And now they were all chasing him.

Tovi ducked as antlers swept past, gouging bark from a tree. A Gornian lunged, snapping at his satchel, teeth tearing at the strap. He yanked it free, dirt exploding under his boots.

"No, no, no—this isn't the experiment!" he shouted, though no one could hear him but the monsters. "This isn't the test!"

The herd roared back, as if mocking him.

He ran harder. His lungs burned, his legs screamed, but instinct kept him moving. The forest blurred—moonlight flashing through the canopy, trees whipping past in streaks of shadow and silver. Every breath was fire.

The Rampiro thundered behind him, the Gornians shrieked, the ground itself seemed to crack beneath the stampede.

The world had collapsed into thunder.

Tovi's head rang from the impact of the other boy's shoulder. His glasses were crooked again, his strap leaning from near-death brushes with the Gornians attempted clawings, and his notes scattered like pale leaves into the stampede's wake. He clawed after a page, only for a hoof the size of a bucket to smash it into pulp.

No saving them now.

A Rampiro bull thundered past so close its antlers sliced the bark from a tree. Tovi flinched, the scream lodged in his throat. Then the boy, knife flashing, shoved him aside, sparing him from being skewered.

"Are you trying to get us killed?!" Tovi shouted, voice cracking with terror.

"I was doing fine until you showed up!" the boy shot back, hair wild, eyes blazing. His bravado was absurd, heroic in a doomed kind of way, but absurd.

Another Gornian lunged from behind, claws slashing. Tovi shoved the boy forward, the motion instinctive. Claws ripped dirt instead of flesh and his stomach lurched with horror. He'd just saved a stranger with the same recklessness that had doomed him tonight.

The Rampiro herd surged faster, their bodies battering trees into splinters. Gornians swarmed in, weaving between legs, snapping at calves and at them. The boy slashed at one of the beasts and actually drove it back. Tovi was in momentary awe. Then reality slammed harder: this was his fault. He'd spooked the bull. He'd triggered the stampede. Without him, maybe none of this would be happening.

But he couldn't admit that. Not now.

"Run!" he screamed instead, voice tearing out of him.

"I am running!" the boy snapped, already barreling forward like the chaos only fueled him.

Tovi ran too, lungs searing, legs heavy as lead. The two of them dodged antlers and tails, stumbling in sync, shoved together by terror. The noise battered him—Rampiro bellows, Gornians shrieks, hooves like hammers. Moonlight flickered through the branches, strobe-flashing the madness around them.

At one point the boy glanced over, their eyes meeting. His burned with reckless fire. Tovi's burned with fear. But both were alive, and both refused to stop.

Chapter 5
Escape?

The forest howled with death.

The Rampiro herd thundered like a living avalanche, their hooves cracking roots into splinters, antlers cleaving through trees. Their bellowing roars shook the canopy, sending birds scattering in frantic waves. Every beast was a moving mountain, blind with panic, unstoppable once in motion.

Weaving between their legs came the Gornians, sleek shadows with glinting teeth, their tails slashing like whips. They darted in and out of the herd, snapping at flanks, shrieking in triumph whenever a calf stumbled. Their eyes burned with hunger. This was their feast.

And in the middle of it, two boys ran for their lives.

Jax barreled forward, knife clutched tight, lungs heaving. His arms ached, his legs burned, but stopping wasn't an option. Tovi stumbled at his side, clutching at the half empty jar of meth in his satchel. Smearing each stone and tree he touched, he hoped it would disuade the Gornians from their pursuit.

Every other step he tripped, only to be yanked upright by Jax's impatient shove.

"Keep up!" Jax roared, slashing at a Gornian that lunged from the left.

"I'm trying to help!" Tovi gasped, nearly tripping on a root. "You think I planned this?!"

"Could've fooled me!" Jax spat, ducking as a Rampiro's antlers sheared the branches above them clean. Leaves rained down in a glittering spray.

The herd pressed closer, the Gornians snapping at their heels. The boys darted left, only to be cut off by another wave of beasts crashing through the trees. Right was no better; more bodies, more horns. There was no clear path, only chaos.

A Gornian burst from the brush, jaws snapping. Jax swung his knife, but the beast was too quick. Its claws raked across his forearm, hot pain flaring. He stumbled, blood dripping into the dirt.

"No!" Tovi shouted, panic sharp in his voice. He hurled a fistful of crushed menth-leaf into the air. The scent made the Gornian recoil with a hiss, but only for a second.

"Go!" Jax snarled, grabbing Tovi by the sleeve and dragging him forward.

The ground tilted suddenly; no, not tilted. Collapsed. A Rampiro bull plowed into a rotten trunk, the tree toppling with a crash that sent the forest floor trembling. Dirt exploded around them, the air filling with dust and splinters.

The boys dove, rolling into a shallow gulley as the herd thundered past overhead. Hooves slammed the earth above like war drums. The noise was deafening, the ground shaking as though the world itself might split apart.

"Stay down!" Jax barked, pressing himself flat against the earth.

Tovi obeyed, trembling, his face half-buried in mud. The Rampiro stormed over them, their shadows blotting out the moonlight, their bellows rattling his ribs. He was certain they'd be trampled into nothing.

Then the herd surged onward, leaving broken trees and churned earth in their wake.

The boys staggered upright, coughing, mud streaking their faces. For a moment, the world seemed still again.

Then the Gornians found them.

Four of the reptilian beasts slithered down into the gulley, eyes glowing, teeth bared. Their tails lashed the dirt, their throats rattling with hungry growls.

"Great," Jax muttered, wiping blood from his arm. "Round two."

Tovi's pulse spiked. He had no weapon but his herbs and his wits. He fumbled for another sprig of menth, his hands shaking violently.

The lead Gornian lunged, and Jax shoved Tovi back, slashing upward with his knife. Steel skittered across scale, the blade peeling a shallow line of scales from its snout. The beast recoiled, shrieking, but the others darted in from the sides.

Tovi flung the crushed herb into one's face. It hissed, clawing at its muzzle, but the others pressed closer, unbothered.

"They're not stopping!" Tovi cried.

"Then let's move!" Jax roared, grabbing his sleeve.

They bolted from the gulley, scrambling up the dirt bank, branches straining at their clothes to hold them captive. Behind them, the Gornians shrieked, claws scrabbling on stone as they gave chase.

The forest became a blur of silver moonlight and black shadows. The boys crashed through brush, dodged roots, vaulted fallen logs. Every breath was fire, every step a gamble between survival and death.

Somewhere ahead, the roar of water reached their ears. A stream.

"This way!" Tovi shouted, his voice breaking.

They stumbled into a shallow riverbed, icy water splashing up their legs. The Gornians skidding at the bank, hissing in frustration. For a moment, they hesitated, claws raking the dirt, eyes gleaming. Then the largest leapt into the water with a splash.

"Keep moving!" Jax shouted, dragging Tovi downstream.

The current tugged at their boots, slippery rocks trying to topple them. Water roared louder as the stream bent toward a drop.

Tovi's heart stopped. "That's a..."

"Don't care, keep going!" Jax bellowed.

The stream cascaded over a jagged ledge, crashing into a pool below. The boys had no choice. They plunged over the edge, the world spinning in a blur of spray and moonlight.

They hit the pool hard, water swallowing them whole. Cold stabbed their skin like knives. Tovi thrashed, struggling to find the surface. Then a hand grabbed his collar; Jax, dragging him up, hauling him into the shallows.

They collapsed on the rocky shore, coughing, gasping, every muscle screaming.

Down the bank behind them, the Gornians shrieked, circling at the bank above, unwilling to leap into the drop. Their eyes glowed like coals in the dark as they slunk back into the trees.

The Rampiro bellows faded into the night; the forest falling back into quiet, save for the rush of the waterfall.

The boys lay side by side, panting and shivering; their eyes locked on the heavens above the broken canopy. The silence didn't feel like safety; it felt like disbelief.

Jax spat water, still clutching his knife with a trembling fist.

"Well... that was fun."

Tovi barked a laugh that was half a sob. "You're insane."

Coughing out the last of water Jax gave him a thumbs up. "You're welcome."

The tremors reached Hreli before the sound did.

The earth quivered underfoot, rattling tools against walls, spilling baskets of grain. Chickens scattered in a frenzy, dogs barked in alarm. Villagers looked up from fields and porches, eyes wide, hands tightening around hoes, rakes, and pitchforks.

Then the sound came. A low, rolling thunder that grew with each heartbeat. A chorus of bellows that shook the air, a storm of bodies barreling closer.

"Rampiro," someone whispered.

The call spread like wildfire. "Rampiro Stampede!"

Men and women scrambled, shouting to pull children inside. Hunters rushed for their bows, though all knew it was folly—no weapon could stop a herd once it was moving. The best they could do was guide the panic, keep it from flattening the village whole.

At the Renner home, Jax's mother threw open the door, voice sharp with fear. "Jax! Inside, now!"

But the house was too quiet. His bed, untouched. His boots...gone.

Her breath hitched.

"Derrek," she whispered.

Jax's father, broad-shouldered and weary from the harvest, stepped in behind her. His eyes flicked to the empty bed, then to the trembling lantern on the table. His face hardened.

"He's not here."

Panic flared in her eyes.

"Where...?"

"Later." His voice was grim, steady. He grabbed the heavy scythe leaning against the wall, knuckles white around the handle. "Right now, we get people to safety."

The ground shook harder. Dust drifted from the rafters. The first Rampiro bellow cracked the night air like thunder.

Across the fields, silhouettes loomed; antlers wide as branches, bodies massive as wagons, eyes rolling wide with that initial fear. They crashed through the treeline in a storm of muscle and horn, tearing up fences like paper.

"Hurry!" the hunters roared.

Fences shattered, wood flying. Rampiro thundered through the crops, trampling furrows flat. Grain scattered into the air like sparks. A house wall cracked against the panicked beasts slamming; children screaming inside until neighbors dragged them out.

And in the middle of the chaos, Derrek Renner was there.

He swung the scythe at snapping Gornians that darted in behind the herd, keeping them from the wounded. He shouted orders, guiding villagers to higher ground, shielding others with his broad frame. His voice cut through the panic, steady, commanding.

Then the herd split.

A bull, larger than the rest, barreled down the lane, its antlers wide as a cart, its bellow drowning out the shouts of fleeing villagers. Dirt sprayed from its hooves, each step pounding the earth like a war drum.

Derrek Renner stood his ground. His scythe gleamed in the moonlight, both hands gripping the haft harder. His chest heaved once, steadying.

Then...his Band lit.

A hard, golden glow seared against his wrist, brighter than any lantern. The crowd gasped. The light wrapped around him in threads of fire, sinking into his arms, his chest, his legs. The air vibrated with the sudden surge of power, the crackle of strength magnified.

Derrek roared. His muscles corded, the ground splintering beneath his boots as he braced himself. With impossible speed, he swung the scythe upward, the blade singing through the air like a crescent moon.

For one breathtaking moment, the Rampiro faltered. Its head snapped right, antlers tearing through the dirt instead of the village homes. A near-miss. Villagers shouted in awe.

But the beast was too massive. Too furious.

The glow from Derrek's Band sputtered, flickered, and went dark. His breath caught, the strain bending him low. The Rampiro bull bellowed and surged again, this time unstoppable.

The last thing his wife saw was the light dying on his wrist as the storm of antlers and muscle engulfed him.

The hole beneath the tree roots was barely big enough for two. Its walls pressed close, damp earth against their backs, roots dangling like ribs from the broken trunk. Water still dripped from their hair, pooling in the mud at their knees.

Jax leaned against the wall, chest heaving, his arms and back slick with blood where claws had raked him. The gash burned with every twitch and movement; an irony musk, filling their small hideout.. He pressed a hand to the wound, hissing, but there was nothing to wrap it with. Nothing to stop the slow trickle.

Beside him, the other boy slumped forward, glasses cracked, satchel torn open at his side. His hands shook as he tried to scoop loose scraps of paper back into it, though some of the charcoal markings were already smeared beyond saving.

Neither spoke at first. The rush of the river outside, their only ambience.

Then Jax's eyes caught the paint.

Bold ochre slashes marked his own shoulder and chest—Hreli's pride, mimicking Rampiro antlers. But when he looked at the other boy, he saw the thin green-black streaks along his jawline, curling sharp against pale skin. Fang-lines.

Wihflan.

Jax's lip curled.

The boy shrank under his stare, gaze flicking to Jax's markings, before his expression hardened with equal disdain.

Of course. Two villages, two rivals. Rampiro hunters and Gornian stalkers, thrown into the same chaotic maelstrom.

"Well," Jax muttered, his voice rough, "that explains a lot."

The boy pushed his glasses higher, though the crack made them sit crooked. "What's that supposed to mean?"

"Figures one of you would run headfirst into a herd and ruin everything."

The boy scoffed, hugging his ruined bag tighter.

"Better than charging at Gornians with a knife you can't keep a hold of!"

Jax bristled but didn't argue. His arm throbbed, lungs still raged against him. Instead, he tilted his head back against the dirt wall, shutting his eyes. "Doesn't matter. We're alive."

The words just lingered there, heavy with what they weren't saying.

Jax thought of the moment in the river when he'd yanked the other boy up from the current. He could've sworn his Band had a sputtering flicker, a faint glow before the plunge snuffed it out. He hadn't dared look again.

The boy thought of the Rampiro antlers, the shove that had knocked him clear. In that instant, his own Band had pulsed too, a faint throbbing of light. He rubbed at his wrist now, half-convinced it was just moonlight reflecting off the wet skin.

Neither spoke of it.

Outside, the forest creaked as the last of the herd's thunder rolled away. The Gornians' shrieks faded into the distance, their hunt carrying them elsewhere. The river ran steady and cold.

In the hollow, two boys sat shoulder to shoulder, bruised, bleeding, dripping mud, and glaring at one another with mistrust.

But neither moved away.

For all their bitterness, they both knew the same truth:

Whatever they had unleashed, they would not survive a second wave alone.

Chapter 6
The Pact of Zeros

Dawn came like a bruise, purple and sore along the treetops.

The cacophony caused by the beasts had moved on in the night, leaving the forest in a stunned hush. Where the herd had passed, trees leaned at odd angles, those that hadn't been sheered in half, and saplings lay snapped like kindling. The ground was a churned mess of hoof-punched mud, gouged roots, and torn shrubs slick with crushed leaves. Every so often a branch cracked somewhere far off, the last groan of a trunk that hadn't quite decided whether to stand or fall.

The two boys pulled themselves out of the hole where they'd found refuge.

Jax grimaced as he climbed out. His mud-slicked hair caked into the tattered remains of his shirt. Dried brown smears striped his back and forearm where claws had raked him. Blood still seeped in thin, stubborn lines, sticky where dirt had mingled overnight. He pressed his palm over parts of the wound, teeth clenched, and kept moving.

Tovi stumbled after him, glasses cracked, satchel hanging by a single thread of leather. Soggy pages flopped out as he walked, sticking to his tunic like limp leaves. He tugged them free, winced, and stuffed them back again as if that could un-ruin them. His breath rasped in short, panicked pulls that he tried to quiet, but the quiet made everything louder.

They reached a wind-felled trunk and slumped against it. The river they'd escaped through whispered behind them, the only sound brave enough to keep going.

Jax tilted his head and spat mud from the corner of his mouth. His eyes kept darting to the shadows like he expected teeth to come flicking out of them. When his gaze slid, it snagged on the thin green-black streaks painted along the other boy's jawline.

Of course the forest had decided they deserved each other.

A breeze lifted the reek of trampled greenery, and Jax's hand drifted to his wound again, hissing at the slightest touch of the raw ridges. He started tearing at the cloth now dried to his skin, deepening some of the wounds.

"Don't," Tovi said, voice rough. He didn't look at him when he said it. "If they catch the scent, they'll come back."

His mouth pressed into a thin line. The sudden bravado scaring even himself, he tucked his hands beneath his elbows.

They pushed on.

Walking hurt, but stopping hurt too. Either way, pain had hands on their shoulders and pushed. They followed the broken lane the herd had carved, threading between splintered trunks and islands of untouched fern as if stepping through the ribs of something gigantic. Birds had begun to test the morning with uncertain chirps. When a magpie landed on a bent branch, they both flinched hard enough to startle it into flight again.

At a shallow rise where the ground wasn't chewed to paste, Jax faltered. He braced one palm on his knee and drifted toward sitting without quite meaning to. Tovi hovered, awkward as a foal, then sank beside him because there wasn't anywhere else to be.

They didn't look at each other. They looked at their hands, at the ragged edges of their sleeves, at the way dawn light caught on suspended droplets in a spiderweb strung between two broken stems. The web swayed. The beads slid. Somewhere, water dripped in a patient rhythm.

"Your... shoulder," Tovi said at last, not quite a question.

Jax grunted in agony. Tovi looked around and then tore a strip from the inside hem of his tunic, twisting and tying it into a knot with his left hand. It was clumsy work

"Here," Tovi said, reaching before he could stop himself.

Jax flinched and so did Tovi. His fingers hovered, then settled. He didn't tie a neat healer's bandage, it was a kid's knot, the kind you use when you've never had to learn better and now you wish you had. A sling, ugly but useful.

A faint warmth engulfed both their wrists, as a ripple of light, there, but not there. They both glanced down, startled, then away, pretending it was only the way the new day's sun hit damp skin.

Jax rolled his shoulder carefully adjusting himself within the makeshift wrappings. Pain flared; then steadied.

"Thanks," he said, forcing himself back to his feet, as if it might keep the forest from noticing how shaky his hands were.

Tovi tucked his ruined pages deeper into his satchel, as if hiding them might make them less ruined. He traced the corner of a chart he'd redrawn so many times the paper had thinned. There was a hole where numbers should have been. He could feel the exact shape of it with his fingertip.

A low groan rippled through the trees ahead, like a door somewhere in the woods was being slowly opened. The boys jerked upright. Jax reached for the knife at his hip and Tovi's breath hitched. They waited, pinned to stillness by the sound.

It was only the forest settling. The groan faded and the birds, heartened by not being stomped into silence, sang with braver chirps.

They stood. Not because they were ready, but because staying put felt like asking to become a small, neat pile of bones for something else to find later.

The path tipped down toward a shallow ravine. On the far lip, the trees thinned, revealing a sliver of sky bruised from purple to pink. Jax set his jaw and started down, boots sliding in ruts where hooves had churned mud. Tovi followed, one hand out to balance, the other clutching his sack's strap that squeaked in protest with every step. Twice, he slipped. Twice, a rough hand caught his elbow, hauled him upright without words. The second time, he mumbled something that could have been thanks.

"Keep your head low," Jax said, still not looking back. "If the horns come, you won't have time to duck."

"You think they'll circle back?" Tovi asked, voice cracking high and tired.

"I don't know what anything will do anymore."

At the bottom of the ravine lay a puddled ribbon of brown water and a mess of tracks: Rampiro hooves punched deep; Gornians claws etched between. The boys paused on the lip and stared. Jax crouched and put his hand in the print of a hoof. It swallowed his palm. He pulled back quickly, as if touching it might summon the thing that made it.

On the climb up, his legs trembled, buckling at one point. Tovi's hand pressed once against his back; a quick steadying. Then retracted as if embarrassed by its own kindness. Another soft flicker across two Bands, gone as fas as it had come.

They topped the ridge, and the forest fell away in torn strips. The world beyond sloped into fields and fences, and farther still, where the morning mist lay in low pools, something like the faint suggestion of roofs. Smoke rose there, thin and wavering.

Jax stopped and Tovi almost ran into him.

He didn't move. Didn't breathe. The ochre paint at his shoulder looked darker in the new light. Wihflan green-black and Hreli red stood side by side; neither able to voice the sight before them.

A crow landed on a broken fencepost ahead and gave one harsh caw, like a bell struck with a stone.

The neat fields Jax had grown up running through were torn into a battlefield. Rows of grain lay flattened, trampled into brown paste. Fences sagged or lay shattered outright, splinters jutting from the mud like broken teeth. One of the outlying huts had its wall caved in, smoke leaking from a cooking fire overturned in the chaos.

Villagers swarmed the ruins. Men strained to right carts and drag Rampiro carcasses off paths. Women pressed rags to wounds, their hands soaked crimson as they worked in frantic rhythm. A boy Jax's age limped past with his leg bound in a bloody strip of cloth, teeth gritted against the pain. Children clung to doorframes, wide-eyed and silent, while their painted brows streaked with tears.

The scent was worse than the sight. Trampled earth, crushed herbs, the sharp tang of blood, human and beast alike.

Jax's gut twisted. This wasn't just the aftermath of a herd. This was punishment.

Beside him, the other boy stiffened. His cracked glasses reflected the fires as he clutched his satchel close. The black fang marks at his jawline all but glared in the light. Wihflan. Wrong place, wrong tribe.

Heads turned. Murmurs rose. The crowd looked toward them; mud-caked, battered, one bleeding, one branded with rival paint. Suspicion burned hotter than the hearth fires.

"Derrek's brat brought home a Wihflan?"

"Look at his markings!"

"Search his bag! What's he carrying?"

A rough hand grabbed for Tovi's shoulder. He jerked back, nearly losing his satchel. Another man stepped forward, hand outstretched to seize it.

Jax moved without thinking. He shoved himself between them, squaring his battered frame, blood still seeping from his arm. His glare swept across faces he'd known since he was small—men who'd carried him on their shoulders after hunts, women who'd pressed sweets into his palm during festivals. He felt their judgment like knives.

"Back off," he snapped, voice hoarse but sharp enough to still them. "He's with me."

A hush spread, brittle and dangerous.

"With you?" one villager barked. "That's Wihflan paint he wears."

Another spat into the mud. "You drag an enemy here, after this? Look at what's been done!" He gestured wide, to the wreckage of their fields, the torn earth, the groans of the injured.

Jax's throat closed. The scene pressed harder than the bandage-less gash on his arm. He wanted to shout that it hadn't been like this when he'd gone into the woods—that it wasn't supposed to be like this at all. But the memory of horns, claws, and thunder smothered the words.

Instead, he threw out the only truth he had: "He saved me."

The words rang out, and the crowd's reaction was immediate. Gasps, laughter, scoffs.

"Saved? By a Wihflan?"

"Pathetic."

"Rather be dead than owe them."

Anger flared across Jax's brow, shame biting deep, but he didn't flinch. "Laugh if you want," he shouted back, voice breaking. "But I'm alive because of him. And that matters."

Tovi blinked at him, startled.

The villagers stared. Then Jax turned, chest still heaving, and faced him. "What's your name?"

Tovi hesitated. His eyes flicked between Jax, the angry crowd, and the broken fields. For a moment, it seemed like he might stay silent. Then his shoulders straightened, thin but stubborn.

"...Tovi," he said, voice quiet but clear. "Tovi Keldrin."

Jax nodded once, firm, and extended his arm; Hreli markings showing through the grime.

"Jax. Jax Renner."

Tovi shifted his satchel to one side, lifted his own arm, and met him. Their forearms locked in the warrior's clasp, not a boyish game, but a battered bond of survivors.

The crowd groaned, but no one pressed closer.

Somewhere deeper in the village, a woman's wail carried on the winds, sharp with grief. The sound cut through Jax like a blade, but he forced himself not to turn, not to ask.

The clasp broke. Their hands dropped to their sides.

Jax had chosen.

And if the cost of that choice came later, he would carry it alone.

Chapter 7
No More

V illagers turned back to their work, but not without snide remarks; words that could wound. A woman gathering spilled grain glanced once more at Tovi, shaking her head. A group of hunters dragging a Rampiro hide snorting...

"Saved by a Wihflan. No wonder he's still a zero."

"His father must be ashamed."

"Dead weight, both of them."

Jax's jaw clenched until it hurt. Every word bit, but he forced his shoulders square, his feet planted in the churned mud. He wanted to shout back, to swing the knife still at his belt, to make them see what it had taken just to get back here alive. But no roar came. His throat was raw, his breath still labored.

Somewhere to the left, near the broken fence line, two voices whispered low.

"Derrek didn't make it.""Made a stand against the biggest bull to keep some of the others from safe...""Yea he got a good hit in, but that was old Brutus...."

The words slid under Jax's skin like barbs. His head whipped toward them, but the men had already bent back to their work, hauling fence-posts upright.

The world tilted for a moment. His vision blurred, the words slamming into him so hard he staggered. Brutus was legendary among the hunters. The leader of the herd for over eight decades, he was massive even by Rampiro standards. Jax dug his nails into his palm until pain steadied him. He couldn't break, not in front of all these people. If he broke now, they would all see. And he could not let them.

So he shoved it down, buried it deep under rage and shame, where no one else could touch it. His father's name burned behind his teeth, unsaid.

Instead, he threw words back at the crowd, voice harsh enough to scrape: "He saved me!"

It wasn't just defiance anymore. It was armor.

The villagers froze again, eyes narrowing on Tovi.

"You mean him?" someone spat. "The fang-marked boy?"

"Yes, him!" Jax's voice cracked, but he didn't care. "Mock me if you want, but I'd be bones in the forest if he hadn't distracted the Gornians. That's truth. And I'll say it again if I have to."

Laughter rippled through the crowd, bitter and cold.

"Imagine bragging about that."

"Hreli's zero, dragged back to life by Wihflan's runt."

"Better to die a man than live like that."

The words bit more because they carried some truth. Jax's face flushed, shame boiling under his skin, but he didn't move. If they thought they could laugh him into silence, they were wrong.

Beside him, Tovi shrank under their glares. His cracked glasses caught the firelight; hands clutching the strap so tight his knuckles bleached white. For a moment, he looked like he might vanish into himself completely, until his gaze met Jax's.

There was no gratitude in it. No warmth. Just shock and the realization that Jax had tied their fates together in front of everyone.

The murmurs dulled as villagers drifted back to their work. Not convinced. Not forgiving. But too burdened with mending fences, binding wounds, and counting losses to keep circling the boys.

A child cried for his mother. A woman wailed from somewhere deeper in the village, raw and ragged. The sound made Jax's stomach twist, but he kept his face carved in stone. He didn't ask who. He already knew.

By the time the square thinned, the two of them stood alone near the shattered cart. The the villager's eyes, even when turned away, still lingered on them like smoke that refused to clear.

Jax couldn't help but clutch at his chest, a hollow unease worming it's way into his core.

His arms heavy, his legs moving without asking. He pushed through the square, past villagers who turned away or muttered sharp words under their breath. The world blurred at the edges, but he followed the path he knew by heart—the one that led home.

The lane looked wrong. Fences he and his father had mended last season were splintered again, posts jagged like broken teeth. A cart lay half-buried in mud, wheels cracked, the last of its load scattered and ruined. Chickens scratched aimlessly near spilled grain, their soft clucks a mockery of the recent fiasco.

Jax's boots sank deep into the trampled ground as he reached the plot. Baskets were crushed flat, stalks of grain matted into the mud, soaked with hoofprints and blood. A strip of cloth dangled from the axle, his father's work sash, torn in half.

Two neighbors worked nearby, setting aside what little grain could be salvaged. Seeing Jax, their movements slowed. One opened his mouth, then stopped. The other's voice came out rough, like the words had to be dragged:

"Derrek didn't make it, Jax. I'm... sorry."

The air collapsed in Jax's lungs. He staggered, catching the wall of the hut with his hand before his knees gave out. His ears roared, drowning everything else, but the words kept echoing anyway. Didn't make it. Trampled. Gone.

The men bent back to their work, leaving him with the broken cart and the strip of cloth swaying in the dawn breeze.

Jax crouched. His fingers brushed the sash, rough with dirt and blood. He let his palm rest there, trembling, as if maybe warmth still lingered. His throat ached with words that wouldn't form. Apologies. Pleas. Promises. None made it past his teeth.

The only thing that slipped out was a whisper, so quiet even the wind almost missed it.

"My fault."

The words lodged in his throat, thick as dry bread. He pressed them down, locking them away, because if he let them grow roots he'd never stand again.

He went inside. The hut smelled of smoke and earth, a place built from sweat and stubborn hands. His mother's blanket was folded neatly in the corner; she must have gone to tend the wounded. His father's chair sat empty by the hearth.

Jax's eyes landed on the pair of blades hanging above the cot. He pulled them down, the familiar weight sharp in his hand. He remembered the day his father had finally let him hold them.

"A blade's only as good as the hand that holds it. Don't forget that."

Now the words pierced his heart, a testament to his lack of strength, his lack of foresight, his lack of...

He gathered what he could. A satchel. A heel of bread. A canteen, half full. He paused at his cot, staring at the rough blanket, the worn wood frame. The thought of sinking into it and never getting up, crossed his mind. Instead, he turned away.

When he stepped back into the light, the pack was slung across his shoulder. His Band at his wrist stayed dull, lifeless, but he clenched his fist around it. Something in him hardened. He had to atone and he would not do that staying here. He could not.

His feet carried him back through the wreckage, past the villagers who gave him side-eyes and murmured about curses and zeros. Past the children peeking from door-ways, whispering his name like it was already a warning.

Crossing the village's outer fence, he found Tovi. The Wihflan boy stood stiff, two hunters lingering nearby with suspicion in their eyes.

Jax dug into his pack, pressing the bread into Tovi's hands. "Go home," he snorted, voice rough.

Tovi blinked. "What?"

"Back to Wihflan. You don't belong here." Jax's hand lingered on the loaf, then dropped. He adjusted his own pack higher on his shoulder and turned toward the road that wound away from Hreli.

The hunters exchanged looks but didn't move. Tovi clutched the satchel, staring at Jax's back as he started forward. His lips parted, but no words came out.

The path stretched ahead, faint and uneven, fading into the distance. Jax's boots pressed into it one step at a time, his breath ragged growing more ragged. Behind him, Hreli groaned with the judgement of his actions; his mother's voice carried in a cry he refused to turn toward.

He kept walking.

And the boy behind him, silent and uncertain, kept staring after him.

Chapter 8
Forked Roads

Jax walked. It was the only thing he knew to do. The dirt road stretched out before him in a pale ribbon, winding between fields torn raw by the stampede. Every step carried him farther from Hreli, but no matter how far he pushed himself, the destruction of the village clung to his shoulders like chains.

He hadn't even gone back to the square to say goodbye, taking back alleys to circumvent any interactions. He couldn't bare the look in their eyes; the mix of scorn and pity, still scraped at him like the Gornians' claws. Every whispered word rang in his ears: Zero… pathetic… better to die than owe Wihflan. And beneath it all, the cry of grief that had split the morning skies when the truth reached the others. His father. His father, crushed under the same thunder Jax had chased as though it were glory waiting to be claimed.

His jaw tightened until his teeth ached but he wouldn't cry. Not until the ground swallowed him whole where no one could see.

"City," he strained, throat raw. The word a scalding totem, a vow. "I'll get to the city. I'll prove it wasn't for nothing."

The claw marks through his arms pulsed with heat. He flexed his fingers against the pain, but the motion only sent fire licking through his shoulder. He pulled the torn cloth of the sling tighter around it, hoping the pressure would help. It didn't. The wound was worse than he wanted to admit. Every beat of his heart felt like a hammer against it, swelling and throbbing.

The road bent through a stretch of withered brush. Birds startled at his passage, scattered with shrill cries. Jax kept walking, forcing his legs forward. If he stopped, he'd think. And if he thought, he'd picture his father's last moments, caught out in the fields facing off against Brutus, while trying to save some village kid or woman. No weapon, no warning, nothing but hooves and horns and terror. The harder the thought clawed at him, the faster he walked.

By the fourth mile his breath came ragged. By the sixth, sweat plastered his hair to his forehead, even though the air had cooled. He yanked at his collar, gasping. Fever was attempting to consume him, riding his bloodstream as surely as the Gornians had driven the herd. His vision swam at the edges, trees bending in and out of shape as though they'd joined the stampede too.

"Not... stopping," he hissed, though his knees buckled, the heat exacerbating symptoms he had yet to accept. He caught himself on a fence post, wood rough under his palms, splinters biting his skin. The farm beyond flattened, crops ground to mush beneath Rampiro hooves. A child's toy, a carved wooden ox, sat broken in the mud. Jax looked at it, eyes glossing as he did; his throat closing until he shoved himself back onto the road.

He hated how the fever was warping the world around him. The shadows whispered, turning tree limbs into antlers, hollow trunks into glaring eyes. Sometimes, he swore he saw his father's broad back ahead of him on the path, baskets balanced across his shoulders. But when he blinked, the image crumbled, leaving only dust and pain behind.

By late afternoon, Jax's bravado had thinned to raw instinct. He was half-limping now, his arm swollen, the makeshift bandage soaked through again and again. Flies buzzed at it, and he snarled, swatting them away. His stomach churned with hunger, but the thought of food made bile rise. He had long since drained the half full canteen.

"Hero's life," he whispered hoarsely, dragging his feet along. "Yeah. Great start."

The path ahead dipped into a shallow ravine where the road narrowed between jutting rocks. He staggered down the slope, one hand dragging across stone to keep upright. The world tilted, and he dropped to one knee, then another, the knife at his belt digging into his hip as he pitched forward. He tried to catch himself, but the sudden weight tore at his wound, and the scream that escaped sounded like a dying beast.

Jax didn't get back up.

Laying there, pressed against the dirt, his breaths came in distressed, uneven gasps. Sweat dripped into his eyes, stinging as they traced cuts along their paths. He clawed weakly at the road, dragging himself a few more inches, then stopped. His body wasn't his anymore; it was lead, molten and heavy, sinking him down.

The fever had taken him. Trees blurred into the shadows of Rampiro horns. Minute breezes seemed to howl with his father's voice. The dirt beneath his cheek shuddered with phantom hoofbeats; holding him hostage as curdled, broken phrases bleed together, their only audience the dust lacing his parched lips. Noises to be forgotten.

The road stretched ahead, uncaring. The sun slid lower, throwing long bars of shadow across his body. Somewhere in the distance, a crow cawed, sharp and mocking.

Jax shut his eyes and let the fever drag him under.

Chapter 9
Return to Wihflan

Wihflan carried the stale vibe of menth smoke and wet leather.

Tovi crossed the narrow bridge where the creek pinched the village into two cramped halves, the boards worn smooth by years of quick feet and quicker choices. Houses leaned close together, rooftops stitched with rawhide, their shadows falling in long, sharp triangles that cut the lane into pieces. Hunters moved like rumors along the alleys; light steps, soft voices, black fang-marks painted across cheekbones and jaws. No one stopped him. Plenty stared.

He kept his eyes on the ground, on the places where the shale poked through the dirt like teeth. Every step pulled the night back through his bones; the herd's thunder, the snapping tails, the river swallowing and spitting him out. His satchel tugged at his shoulder, hanging by a restitched strap that didn't trust him any more than the villagers did.

The halfway house squatted at the end of a crooked lane, a slouching building with patched shutters and a door a full hand shorter than it should've been. Someone had painted its lintel with a single, careful line, Wihflan's promise: not family, not forever, but a roof.

Tovi pushed inside.

The common room was full. Children of all ages elbow to elbow playing games, lounging, or doing random chores. A pot hung over the hearth, steam carrying the bitter bite of menth and something starchy. Four boys huddled at the table with carved game tiles, their heads close. They looked up as Tovi entered. Smirks bloomed.

"Look who crawled back," said Bren, the tallest. His fang-mark paint curled up toward his ears, mean as a grin. "Phantom Zero."

Someone snorted. "Lose your charts to the wind again, Tov?" "Maybe the numbers ran faster than he did." Bren chuckled "Maybe the numbers bit him," mocked another.

Tovi shrugged out of his satchel without answering. The strap protested. He set the bag on the floor like it might collapse if he breathed wrong. His legs wanted to give. He locked his knees instead and wiped his cracked glasses with a sleeve that only spread the river-silt around.

Footsteps thumped from the back hall, and Matron Kes appeared; small as a hawk and twice as observant, dark hair braided tight to her head. She took him in with one cut of her gaze: mud, tears tracked clean through it, the ravaged pack. The line of her mouth went flatter.

"You're lucky you weren't carried home on a door," she said. No hello. No are you hurt. "We don't have boards to spare."

"I know," Tovi said. His voice came out lower than he wanted.

She sniffed. "You smell like a river and foolishness boy. Get water. Then sleep. Tomorrow you fetch with the others."

"I can't," he said before he could stop it.

Heads lifted at the table, a tile clacking onto the wood.

Kes's eyes narrowed. "Can't, or won't?"

Tovi glanced at the boys. Four smirks waiting to happen. He swallowed. "I... I need to look in my chest."

"Your chest can wait."

"It can't," he said, surprising himself with the steadiness in his voice. "Please."

A long breath moved through the room. Kes stared at him for a long moment, then jerked her chin toward the sleeping alcove. "Five minutes," she said. "And wash your face before you touch anything, Keldrin."

He ducked down the hall. The sleeping space was a narrow gutter of a room with three cots per wall and pegs driven into the wood above each for treasures small enough to live on a nail. Tovi's cot waited at the end, thin blanket smoothed by habit, the wooden chest beneath it bearing the carved initials of someone who had slept here before him and would sleep here after he was gone.

He slid the chest out, trying to lift the top. The lid stuck; the wood had swelled in the wet months and never quite un-swelled. He pried it up with his nails and stared down at everything he owned.

A folded shirt. A second pair of socks, carefully darned at the toe. A cloth bundle of dried roots he'd picked and labeled and never quite used. A flat tin with a bit of charcoal and a lump of wax. And wrapped in a strip of old green wool, his mother's scarf, the wand.

He unset the scarf with careful fingers. The wood beneath was pale, almost ash-colored, more smooth than polished, a simple spiral carved along its length that caught the light like a vine. He had never dared to raise it higher than the level of his own chest. Sometimes he dreamed of it moving in his hand like it wanted to help; sometimes he dreamed of it swallowing light and leaving him cold.

He didn't remember his mother's face as anything but warmth and freckle-constellations. Remembered her voice, though, singing in the kitchen while the pot steamed, the song stopping mid-note when the door burst wide and the hunters shouted manticore, the world becaming claws and smoke. The wand had been in the scarf on the table.

"If you think he's ready for it, then I agree." his father had said, even as he went out the door with a spear he knew was too short. He's ready?

Tovi stroked the spiral with his thumb. The wood was cool. It didn't flare under his touch, but it hadn't done anything else either over the last few years.

Back in the common room, the boys' croonings picked up. Bren's voice carried. "Maybe the Matron'll pin his charts to the fence so real hunters can track the numbers for him."

Another laugh. Tovi rewrapped the wand calmly, as if his hands weren't shaking. He slid it back into the chest, then out again, then held it a long moment in both palms, before placing it in his satchel. Looking around the room, the laughter of Bren and his cronies pressed a long treaded nerve. Grabbing everything else from the chest he shoved them into his spare bag, along with a few other things from the room.

When he came out, Kes had set a tin cup on the nearest table. "Drink," she said. "Menth-water flushes panic."

He drank, mouth coated with biting leaves and stems, and focused his intent.

"You'll fetch in the morning," she said.

"I won't be here," he said.

The room shifted. Tiles paused mid-finger. Bren's smirk stretched. "Running to one of your forest corners to sulk?" he said.

Tovi wiped his mouth with the back of his hand. "Training in the city," he said, and the word stood up straight between them like a post you lash the rest of you to.

Kes's gaze flared and cooled. "You have nothing," she said. "No coin. No escort. The road is dangerous."

"So does staying." He didn't mean to say it out loud. It felt like stepping past a fence that had always been there and realizing it was only string.

Bren flicked a tile.

"Go on, then. Bring the city our leftovers. See if they'll feed you numbers."

Tovi met Kes's eyes again. He could have begged. He didn't.

"Thank you for the roof," he said.

Her jaw worked once. She nodded, her bird-like features tweaking closer.

"If you're going to be foolish, be fast," she said. "Take the creek path. The ridge bandits sleep heavy when the market's poor."

He nodded. "I'll send…" He stopped. What? A letter? A chart that proved anything? He left the sentence where it belonged: nowhere.

At the door, he hesitated. He turned back to the table, to the boys, to the hearth where the pot breathed menth into the room like a warning.

"If any of you ever get stuck in the dark," he said, surprising himself again, "keep your hands low and your head lower. Horns sweep high."

Bren snorted.

"Listen to the scholar of tripping."

"Yeah," Tovi said. "Do."

Old Marna followed him out the door, reaching into her apron pocket.

"Used to be, Wihflan water ran free to our fields in planting month. Then Hreli's levy rose after a dry year and nobody backed down. One bad season turned into bad blood, and now children inherit fights they never picked."

She pressed a heel of bread into Tovi's hands and turned back into the home.

"You'll need more than one for the journey ahead."

Tovi nodded his thanks, stepping into the lane; the air outside colder than when he first returned. The night had started to fade into a thin gray at the edges, the sky paling where it pressed against the black cut of the roofs. He breathed that air in, filling his lungs with freedom and fear.

He pulled his pack tighter, realigning his glasses to avoid having to look through the cracks. He set his feet toward the creek path Kes had named, where the reeds hissed secrets and the stones took impressions of your steps and kept them. The village drifted behind him in murmurs and smoke and the high, crescendoing song of someone sharpening a blade for morning.

He didn't look back.

The path narrowed, then narrowed again, a thread through low brush that held last night's rain. The scarf-wrapped wand shifted against his ribs when he moved, a quiet tap-tap he could feel through bone. He followed the sound of his own footsteps until the houses thinned to huts, the huts thinned to silhouettes, and the silhouettes sank into the dark. Ahead, the road to the city braided with the creek and peeled away again, a line he could step onto if he didn't let himself think too long.

Chapter 10
Fever on the Road

Jax didn't remember falling. The road rose like a fist, smacked his face, and kept him there. His Band pressed into the mud; his breath rasped in shallow, ragged pulls that fogged the dirt a finger's width from his mouth. Flies worried the torn cloth at his arm. The sun had slid low enough to throw the ditch into blue shadow, and then into shadowed darkness. There he lay, face-down, fingers curled around nothing.

Footsteps, cautious and light, came up the lane. In the dark of night, Tovi almost stepped on him.

He jerked back, heart thudding, one hand clutching for his bag in surprise. For a second, he thought it was a dead hunter, his head swiveling to verify a lack of danger. Then the body groaned, mud cracked at the corner of a mouth, and the face tilted just enough for Tovi to see the features beneath the grime.

"Jax," he breathed.

No answer. Just that labored rasp.

Tovi dropped to his knees. He touched Jax's shoulder and recoiled at the heat radiating through the torn sleeve. The wounds across his back, shoulder, and arm had gone from angry red to shiny, blooms of swollen, callous edges puckering with a sourness that made Tovi's stomach pitch. The makeshift binding now sticking to skin like tar.

He slid his fingers to Jax's neck. Pulse: fast and stuttering. Fever, hard and possibly climbing.

Tovi scanned the road. Empty. No carts, no hunters, only a crow balanced on a fence-post watching with flat interest. The ditch long-grass hissed in the wind as if it disapproved of the entire situation.

"Okay," he stammered. "Ooookay."

He wedged both hands under Jax's shoulder and hip.

"One, two..." he whispered, and heaved.

Jax was heavier than he looked. Tovi got him onto his side, then onto his back, then half-dragged, half-walked him out of the rut and into the grassy underbrush of a Thren-bare tree.

Startled at the motion, Jax let loose a slurred snarl.

"Don't..." His hand flailed weakly, smearing mud across Tovi's sleeve.

"Quiet," Tovi said, more to his own panic than to Jax. "Just be quiet. Alright?"

He propped Jax's head on his rolled cloak, then yanked open the satchel. The familiar odors wafted from the bag; menth, ditchleaf, vine resin, the bitter root Kes always said he measured too many times. His fingers moved on their own: flint, tinder, a handful of dry moss saved for exactly this, cupped against a snapped twig pyramid. The spark caught. A pea-sized flame chewed its way into the twigs and settled to a steady orange breath.

With the fire going, Tovi tore the old binding away in strips, soaking each with water first so it wouldn't rip skin. Jax hissed, moaning short, bitten-off sounds that made Tovi's hands go steadier. He cleaned the edges with boiled water from his cup, blew on the steam until it stopped scalding his fingers, and dabbed until the mud ran thin and the rawness showed clean.

"Hurts," Jax rasped, eyes slitting open. They were unfocused, swimming from heat exhaustion. "You...followed... me...?"

"Ran into you face down on the path, so don't flatter yourself," Tovi said. He mashed menth and ditchleaf together on a flat stone with the butt of his knife, the pulp bleeding green under the pressure. "Now, hold still."

He lifted the paste and pressed it across the wound. Jax jolted like he'd been shocked. "Burns."

"Good," Tovi said. "Means it's working."

He wrapped a clean strip of shirt around the poultice and tied it off with the kind of practice you only get from tending yourself when no one else bothers. Then he set a tin cup by the coals, poured in creek water, and broke a knob of bitter root into it. The smell rose sharp and unkind.

Jax eyed the cup like it might bite him first. "No."

"Yes." Tovi slid an arm under his shoulders and levered him up one careful inch at a time. "Small sips. Don't throw it back or it will come back up."

The first swallow made Jax gag. The second went down with a curse. By the third, the grimace on his face had gone from fury to a kind of miserable acceptance. Tovi kept the cup moving, and when the brew was gone, he chased it with water.

The heat off Jax's skin still felt like a hearth. Tovi laid the back of his fingers to the boy's forehead, to his cheek. Too hot. How long had he walked like this? How far from Hreli had shame and stubbornness hauled him before his body quit?

Jax drifted, surfacing and sinking. Sometimes he groaned words that didn't belong to Tovi: a name said like a cut, a half-formed "sorry," a ragged "should've helped with the cart." Each landed and folded itself away inside Tovi's mind.

He added twigs to the fire, then bigger pieces, building it up just enough to keep off the night chill without painting the road. Shadows stepped into the flames and then stepped out. The crow on the fencepost had gone; crickets and field toads, taking their turn surveying the fields.

Tovi rechecked the bandage. The edges wept a little through the cloth, but the stench had already dulled under the menth's strong scent. Good. He mixed a second poultice anyway, grinding the leaves until his palm tingled.

His satchel shifted against his ribs when he leaned. A gentle rapping at his side. The scarf-wrapped length pressed a line across him, familiar and accusing. He slid the flap aside and looked down at the knot of green wool. He had the mad thought of unwrapping it and raising the wand over Jax's arm, as if the wood might choose now to be brave when he hadn't. As if it might glow or hum or refuse him entirely and prove, once and for all, that he was just a boy with charts pretending he could change the math of the world.

He left the knot tied and kept grinding.

"Why," Jax whispered, words dragging, "didn't... you... leave me?"

Tovi didn't answer right away. He adjusted the cloak under Jax's head, nudged the fire, counted the breaths between each rasp. "Because I was there," he said at last.

Wind ran its fingers through the branches of the Threnbare, making the dry branches clack softly. Somewhere far down the lane, a fox barked once and then thought better of saying anything more. Tovi set the fresh poultice within reach. He dabbed Jax's lips with water, then checked the knot at the bandage again. He let his hand hover over the scarf in the satchel and then drew it back to the work his hands already knew.

Jax's breath hitched, steadied, hitched again. The fever clearly wasn't finished with him.

Tovi fed the fire one thin stick at a time and listened to the road breathe in the dark, counting the beats between the crackle and the rasp, waiting to see which would change first.

The fire shrank and flared as the hours dragged. Tovi kept feeding it slivers of wood, careful not to make it bright enough to catch a hunter's eye on the road. Just enough to hold back the cold. Just enough to keep the shadows from swallowing them whole.

Jax twisted and mumbled in the fever. His body burned like it was trying to tear itself apart. Every so often he jerked, fingers clutching at invisible things, the knife that had slipped from his grip, the herd he'd tried to outrun, maybe faces Tovi didn't recognize. His breath rasped like a saw through wood, rough and uneven. Tovi continued to dab water at his lips, coaxing him to drink whenever the pained moans calmed enough to swallow.

The words that Tovi did recognize, concerned him.

"Cart... finish the harvest..." "Should've been me..." "Father...no, wait..."

Each one made Tovi's throat tighten. He knew what those words sounded like: guilt. The kind that carved at one's soul, deeper than any fever would flesh. But he wouldn't ask or press; especially not in Jax's current condition. He only changed the poultice, wrung out the bandage, crushed fresh menth into pulp until his hands tingled from the oils. Every time he peeled away the old wrap, he prayed the angry red on Jax's body would look a little less swollen, a little less poisoned.

Sometimes it did. Sometimes it didn't.

And then it happened.

As he pressed the newest poultice into place, Jax jolted, half waking, half writhing, and Tovi steadied him, pinning his shoulder against the cloak. In that instant, the Bands at both their wrists flickered. A faint ripple of light that shimmered in unison before it faded into the dark.

Tovi froze. His pulse jumping.

He stared at his Band, then at Jax's. Both were dull again, as empty as before. But he had seen it. Felt it.

"No," he muttered to himself. "That's not how it works. That's not supposed to..."

Jax only groaned and turned his head, still caught in his fever.

Tovi went back to work, though his fingers shook now. He couldn't stop replaying the shimmer, the way it had occurred to both of them. He didn't write it down. He wasn't ready to believe it had happened.

The night was a rhythm of tending: stir the fire, grind the herbs, check the bandage, make him drink. Again and again. Eventually, te satchel strap started to dig into Tovi's shoulder and he finally shrugged it off, setting it by the cloak. The scarf-wrapped bundle inside shifted when he did, knocking softly against the wood.

The wand.

It was louder in the silence than the fire ever was. Louder than Jax's rasping breaths. Every time he bent for herbs, his eyes dragged back to it, the spiral of pale wood peeking out from the green wrap. His mother's. His, now. And still untouched.

He imagined it unwrapped, the firelight tracing the carved vine up its length. He imagined lifting it, speaking no words at all, and the fever breaking like a storm pushed out to sea. He imagined the opposite too: fire leaping wild, or worse, nothing happening at all. Proving he was exactly what everyone said...phantom zero.

Jax croaked, tossing weakly; his arm pulling against the fresh binding. Tovi caught it and held on until the spasm passed. His own hands trembled by the end of it. He set Jax's arm down, then sat back on his heels, staring at the satchel.

"You're supposed to mean something," he whispered to the scarf-wrapped wood. His voice cracked, too small against the night. "So what do you mean?"

No answer, just the fire popping. The wand sat quiet, the scarf's frayed edge glowing orange in the firelight.

Tovi rubbed his eyes. He wasn't going to use it. Not unless the breathing stopped. Not unless the fire went out of Jax completely. He told himself that twice, then again, then stopped counting because the thought wouldn't leave him alone.

He sat cross-legged with his satchel in his lap, pulling free a battered notebook bound with cord. Pages already cluttered with crooked charts and wild formulas, margins crawling with symbols only he understood.

At the top of a blank page, he scrawled:

Hypothesis: XP gained outside combat?

Below it:

No visible tokens. No level ticks. But the light did occur.

He chewed the end of his charcoal stub, tapping it against the page hard enough to smudge. The words felt dangerous, like writing them might summon the scorn of every villager who'd ever laughed at his charts. But he couldn't leave them unwritten.

At the bottom, he added:

Non-combat actions = phantom XP? Ripple dissipates? Where does it go?

The page looked like the scrawlings of a madman.

Tovi shoved the notebook back into the satchel, fingers brushing the scarf-wrapped wand. His hand lingered, and for a moment he thought of his mother. He could almost hear her voice, soft as steam over broth, the words she used to murmur when fever had him shivering as a child:

"Rest, little flame. The world waits for you."

Tovi stretched his back against the tree, staring at Jax until exhaustion pulled him into sleep of his own.

As he did the wand pulsed within its bindings. Jax's pulse steadying in time with the flares; his fevered gasps softened, the heat rolling off him dulled, and his random senseless chattering stilled into steady sleep.

Chapter 11
City on the Horizon

A voice startled Tovi awake; loud, cocky, and very much alive. He blinked blearily only to find Jax, shirt off, doing pushups in the dirt like a man training for a tournament. The bandages still wrapped his arm, but the infection was gone. The skin looked...normal.

"Morning!" Jax grinned through gritted teeth, dropping into another set. "Guess I'm tougher than I thought!"

Tovi sat frozen, his jaw dropping in disbelief.

"What? How? That's not possible?! How did....?"

His hands sprang for the satchel, the scarf still hiding its pale spiral. His mother's words echoed in the back of his mind, "the world waits for you."

"Was that a spell..."

Jax lept to a low branch, grinning through sweat as he cranked out pull-ups, muscles taut.

"What did you say?" Jax barked between reps. "Told you I'd be fine." He dropped into a crouch, wiped his brow, and flashed that reckless grin. "A little Gornian scratch? Please. Takes more than that to stop a hero."

Tovi just stared, satchel heavy across his lap, fingers still pressed against the scarf-wrapped wand.

The notes in his book suddenly felt too small for what had just happened.

After a few meters though, Jax's enthusiasm started to wane. Stumbling once he braced against a tree. White heat knifed his shoulder and the world tilted as he sat back hard, breath hissing from his lungs. The wrap Tovi had insisted be replaced on his ribs, now bled through in a dark flower.

"We're going to have to slow down." Tovi said, checking the binding. Raising a hand to block the sun he glanced in the direction they had rested the night before.

"Looks like you've got two good hours in you, then we stop. No arguing."

Jax swallowed back the pain, nodding. As energetic as he'd been eariler, even his pride had to admit that there hadn't made a full recovery, his fever lapping at him in waves.

For the rest of the morning, they cut their pace by half.

The road widened until walls filled their vision; stone stacked higher than any rampart Jax had ever seen, banners snapping bright against the morning sky. Icrison, the river city.

The closer they came, the louder it grew. Wagons creaked under heaps of iron ore and spices. Traders shouted prices across the dust. A hundred different fragrances tangled in the air: leather, sweat, roasting meat, and even the tang of alchemist powders drifted from crates. Every wrist glowed: faint embers, steady flames, blinding beams. Bands marked everyone; farmhands with single digits, merchants flashing mid-twenties, armored guilders whose wrists burned with numbers Tovi couldn't even comprehend.

Jax slowed only long enough to gawk, mouth half-open.

"Look at them all," he breathed. His Band caught the light for a moment, its single digit still empty.

Tovi adjusted his glasses, throat tight.

"Everyone here has levels. Actual levels." He clutched the satchel closer, notebook digging into his ribs. "We're going to stand out."

They reached the gate where guards checked travelers one by one. Each guard wore his Band exposed, the glow of authority. They were clearly looking at bands for verification. A merchant held up his wrist, digits pulsing green; a caravan leader rolled up her sleeve, the guards nodding her through.

Then it was their turn.

The guard nearest them raised a brow. "Business in Icrison?"

Jax grinned, chest out. "Guild Trials." He thrust his bare wrist forward with more confidence than sense.

The guard leaned closer, and the grin faltered. No glow. No number. Just the empty circlet of the Band. His eyes flicked to Tovi, whose Band was the same dull, unlit bronze.

"Zeroes," the guard groaned. A ripple of laughter and whispers spreading through those in line behind them.

"Children playing at heroes.""Guild Trials? At zero?"

Jax's face reddened, but he didn't drop his arm. "That'll change soon enough."

The guard studied them for a beat longer, then finally waved them through with a grunt. "Not my funeral."

They passed under the archway, the murmur of mockery still buzzing at their backs. But once inside, the world exploded into motion. The moment they cleared the gates, the world opened wider than either of them had ever imagined.

Icrison was alive in a way no village could be. The streets thrummed with people, packed shoulder to shoulder, voices rising in a thousand pitches; vendors hawking wares, guild runners shouting messages, children darting between legs with glowing Bands held high like trophies. Every few steps, something caught the eye: a tailor displaying cloaks embroidered with beast hide; a weaponsmith shouting prices over the clang of his hammer; a bard spinning sparks from his fingertips.

Jax stumbled backward trying to take it all in.

"Look at this place! We're not even at the center yet and there's..." He pointed at a hawker pulling an actual scaled Gornian head from a crate. "They're selling boss trophies on the street! That's insane!"

Tovi stayed close, notebook clutched tight under his arm. His eyes darted, not between stalls, but people. At the glowing numbers shining on their wrists. Everywhere he looked, Bands gleamed with progress:

12, 23, 40. Even the children had 3s and 4s pulsing across their Bands.

The whispers came naturally, rolling through the crowd like part of the market chatter."Guild Trials next week—""Yelmers Doom's recruiters will be watching—""Did you hear? One kid hit Level 7 before twelve. They'll have his name on a banner by sundown."

Tovi's mouth tightened. He didn't write any of it down, but every word carved its place in his mind.

Jax, oblivious to the weight of it, strutted forward like he belonged. "Guild Trials," he repeated under his breath, savoring the words. "That's it. That's our shot."

Tovi shot him a look. "You do realize we're the only ones here without a number, right?"

Jax smirked.

"All that means is we'll make a bigger story when we prove them wrong."

But even he faltered when a passing apprentice, armor gleaming, glanced at their bare Bands and snorted. "Zeros," he laughed to his friend, loud enough to sting.

The laughter followed them down the street.

Jax's grin wavered for a moment. Then he squared his shoulders and kept walking. "Let 'em laugh," he said. "We'll see who's laughing after the Trials."

Tovi's gaze lowered; his hand glancing over the imprint of the wand. He couldn't shake the sense that they were stepping into a place where secrets like his wouldn't survive long.

The closer they drew to the center of Icrison, the more the city seemed to bend around a single point. Roads all angled inward like spokes, carts gave way to streams of people, and above it all a great spire of stone and iron thrust into the sky. At its base sprawled a fortress-like structure wrapped in banners that snapped in the breeze—dark cloth stamped with a sunburst split down the middle by a jagged crack.

Tovi slowed, clutching his satchel closer. "That symbol," he murmured, almost to himself. "That's the mark of Yelmers Doom. They're not just a guild, Jax. They're the guild."

Jax had already thrown his shoulders back, strutting as if the cracked sun itself had been stitched for him. "Perfect. The strongest guild in the biggest city. Where else would we belong?"

The wide steps leading to the guild hall were already crowded. Apprentices in gleaming gear lounged against the rails, trading boasts. Traders hawked charms and whetstones at the base. A group of children played at dueling with wooden sticks, shouting kill-calls and collapsing into the dust while their parents laughed.

For a second, Jax let the sight wash over him. This was what he'd dreamed of—the noise, the life, the way everyone carried themselves as if adventure were stitched into their boots. He could almost feel his Band itching for a glow just by standing here.

Inside, the hall swallowed them whole.

It was vast, three floors open to view, balconies circling upward around a central atrium. Banners of every division hung down: red for combat, blue for magic, green for scouting, gold for leadership. Apprentices and veterans alike crisscrossed the space, Bands gleaming with numbers that caught every light. Some pulsed faintly when names were called at the registry desk. Notices tacked to boards listed quests, Trials, even open challenges for ranking.

Jax gawked, mouth ajar. Tovi, by contrast, was already scanning every board, every posted requirement, fingers twitching like he wanted to start copying everything into his notebook at once.

"Look at them," Jax whispered, pointing at a squad striding past in matching leather armor, numbers gleaming on their Bands. Level 9, Level 10, Level 11. "They're—what—our age?!"

Tovi pointed out, "Not our age. Older by at least three, maybe four years." His eyes narrowed at the glimmering digits. "And if those numbers are accurate, they've already cleared multiple Trials. I need to know how many..."

"Bah, doesn't matter," Jax cut in, puffing his chest. "They just started sooner. We'll catch up. Faster, even."

They reached the long desk where a row of clerks handled a ceaseless line of applicants and reports. The man who waved them forward wore spectacles chained to his collar and the thinnest patience either boy had ever seen.

"Names," he said, not looking up from his ledger.

Jax slapped his palm on the desk. "Jax Renner, soon-to-be hero of Icrison."

The clerk raised a single brow but didn't lift his quill. "And you?"

"...Tovi Keldrin," Tovi said quietly.

"Level?"

Jax grinned, leaning on the counter. "Well, about that—"

The clerk's eyes landed on the bare Bands at their wrists. No glow, no numbers, not even a faint etching. His expression didn't change, but the pause spoke volumes.

"Zero," he said, already turning back to the page. His quill scratched as he wrote it down. "Another pair of Zeros."

Whispers stirred in the line behind them. Someone chuckled, not bothering to hide it.

"Came all this way for that?"

"Should've stayed in their village."

Jax's jaw locked. He fought the urge to whirl on them, to demand a duel right there in the hall. But Tovi's hand brushed his sleeve, giving the smallest shake of his head, and Jax bit it back.

The clerk finally looked up, voice flat but oddly rehearsed.

"Since you're asking without asking: Level 1 buys you night access to North Market and the cheap barracks. Level 2 lets you file a Trial petition without a sponsor. Level 3 unlocks apprentice contracts and healer coverage inside the Arena. Below that? You pay full price and wait your turn... if anyone lets you in line."

The clerk slid them a set of parchment slips.

"Registration complete."

Eyeing the two mud-stained boys in travel cloaks he jerked a thumb over to a wall of missing individuals.

"If you insist on throwing yourselves into humiliation, the Serbalo Arena is where Trials are conducted. Twice a week. Bring coin for the entry fee, and..."

He nudged the slips closer to them.

"...a healer. Next."

They were swept aside by the press of the line, jostled into the current of the hall again.

Jax crumpled the slip in his fist. "Did you hear him? 'Humiliation.' We'll show him. We'll show all of them."

Tovi smoothed his own slip, eyes darting over the glowing ink that listed time, place, rules. His stomach tightened as he read the words Trial of Ascension – Open Entry.

Jax shoved his way back into the atrium's bustle, eyes blazing. "Come on, let's see this Arena for ourselves. If they think Level Zeros can't belong here, we'll prove them wrong..."

He didn't wait for Tovi's reply. His voice carried into the hall, reckless and loud, drawing a few more smirks from the passing apprentices. Tovi followed slower, slip in hand, gaze darting to the distant doors that opened onto a wide avenue leading deeper into the city.

The sound of roaring crowds drifted faintly from that direction, like thunder waiting just beyond the walls.

Chapter 12
The Arena Roars

The road funneled them toward it long before they saw the walls. The noise alone was enough; the crash of voices, the thrum of drums, the way the atmosphere was vibrating with expectation. By the time the arena's massive gates came into view, Jax's grin stretched ear to ear.

The arena loomed like a stone beast crouched in the heart of Icrison. Towers flanked its outer ring, each flying banners emblazoned with the cracked sun of Yelmer's Doom. Iron gates wide enough for a caravan of Rampiro stood open, guards in guild colors waving through streams of citizens eager for the day's spectacle.

"Trials day," Tovi gasped, his eyes daunted by the tide of people surging forward. "We shouldn't..."

"Of course we should," Jax cut him off, already swept up by the crowd. "You hear that? That's glory waiting to happen!"

They pressed through the gates, and the world exploded.

Inside, was a cauldron of noise and color. Stone tiers rose high, packed with thousands of cheering patrons. Sunlight slashed down from the open sky, gleaming off weapons, off Bands, off banners that rippled like fire above the crowd. The air carried the thick scents of roasted meat from vendors, sweat, and steel; dust kicked up from the floor below.

The boys wedged themselves into a gap along the railing, half-hidden behind a stone pillar. Two dirt-smeared kids pressed against the crowd's edge, while everyone's eyes were locked on the arena floor.

The first clash hit like thunder.

Two apprentices charged the sands, one wielding a broadsword that hissed with fire along its edge, the other flinging darts of ice with each flick of her wrist. Sparks showered as steel met frost, every strike ringing against the wards etched into the stone. The air stung cold and hot all at once, and the crowd roared approval with every blow.

Jax's jaw dropped, then split into a grin that raced across his face. "Did you see that?! That's insane! That's exactly what I've been training for!"

Tovi clutched his satchel tighter, squinting through cracked lenses. His notebook was already open.

"Training? That's years of form refinement, see her stance? Her arm position? That's not instinct, that's conditioning." His pen dug deeper with each word. "We don't stand a chance in this state."

Another duel began before the last was even decided. A boy no older than Jax darted towards his opponent with no weapon at all; mid-step, shadows twisting from his feet, rising into the shape of a wolf. It lunged, fangs snapping, forcing his opponent to retreat with a glowing shield. The wolf dissolved when the Band at the boy's wrist dimmed, but the audience's cheer shook the seats underfoot.

"Summons," Tovi stated. "Not true beasts. Constructs. Limited by Band strength..."

"Doesn't matter!" Jax whooped, pounding his fist on the stone. "That was a wolf made of shadow, Tov...uh, whatever-your-name-is! A wolf!"

Tovi shoved his glasses up, annoyed. "Which means he's practiced enough control to split his XP output into two distinct channels. You realize what that implies for..."

The next bout silenced both of them.

A girl raised her staff, and the sand itself obeyed. Spears of stone erupted upward, splitting the floor into jagged teeth. Her opponent vaulted onto one, using the height to drive down with twin blades. They clashed midair, Band resonance flaring so bright Jax had to shield his eyes.

The crowd screamed their names. Names the boys didn't know, but names the city worshipped.

Jax couldn't stop grinning. He leaned so far over the railing that Tovi had to yank him back by the collar. "This is it. This is where heroes are made. The sand, the fire, the cheering...this is home!"

"Home?!" Tovi hissed. "We're intruders. Nobodies. They'd laugh us off the floor before we even drew a breath."

Jax barely heard him. His gaze had locked onto the boy who had conjured the shadow wolf. The apprentice had taken a heavy strike to the ribs, collapsing onto one knee. The arena fell to a hush as the other fighter raised his weapon high.

Before he could stop himself, Jax cupped his hands around his mouth and bellowed, "GET UP! YOU'VE GOT THIS!"

The words cracked like a whip. Heads turned. A few nearby spectators glared at him, annoyed. But down in the sand, the boy flinched, then staggered to his feet. His Band pulsed, light trembling around it, and he lifted his arms again, teeth gritted, ready to fight.

And at Jax's wrist, there was a shimmer.

Not bright. Not strong. But there. A glimmer like a drop of sunlight, gone as quickly as it had come.

Tovi froze mid-scribble. His pen hovered, his breath caught. He'd seen it. He knew he had.

That wasn't supposed to happen.

Jax didn't notice. He was already hammering the rail with his fists, shouting so loud his voice rasped raw. "Yes! That's it! Show them you're not done yet!"

The duel roared back to life, blades clashing, shadows twisting, sand flying. The boy fought on, battered but unbroken, and the crowd's cheer swelled again to match Jax's reckless grin.

Tovi shut his notebook slowly, eyes never leaving Jax's wrist. His heart beat faster, not from the crowds or the duels, but from what he'd just witnessed. Something possibly never measured.

The battles blurred into a storm of color and noise. Serbalo Arena didn't pause; it fed on momentum, hurling one spectacle after another into the pit.

Next came a pair of twins, their Bands glowing in eerie unison. They fought as one, weaving patterns of fire and wind that tangled into a cyclone. Sand rose into the air, spun into glowing streams that lashed their opponent like whips. The crowd chanted their family name, every voice striking in rhythm like the beat of war drums.

Then a girl clad in chain and leather strode out, her weapon nothing but a long whistle carved from bone. One sharp note and the ground trembled. Tunneling from below, a beast surged forth, an armored boar, tusks gleaming, eyes burning red. It barreled through her foe's shield with brute force, the impact sending the other apprentice tumbling. The crowd shrieked approval, feet stomping so hard the stone steps rattled beneath Jax and Tovi.

Jax yelled louder, leaning so far forward the railing cut into his ribs. "That's insane! She brought a boar into the fight! You see that?! We need one of those!"

Tovi shook his head, muttering notes under his breath. "Summoning class... no, beast-bonding. That's a bloodline ability. Rare. Almost impossible for ordinary recruits. Unless..." His pen returned to his hands, scratching out new equations.

The arena flipped again, no time to catch breath. Two boys crashed blades in the center, sparks leaping from each strike. But it wasn't their weapons that stole the audience's breath—it was the shimmer trailing their feet. Each step left behind a faint glow, like fireflies caught mid-dance. Speed-enhancement. Precision footwork made visible, their Bands feeding their bodies in ways Jax had only ever dreamed of.

He slapped the rail, voice raw. "That's it...that's me, that's what I'll have! You see that footwork? That's hero stuff!"

A woman near them chuckled, arms crossed, her own Band gleaming bright green. "Hero stuff? From a couple of Zeros sneaking where they don't belong?"

Jax blinked at her, caught between bristling and fear of getting thrown out. He opened his mouth, but Tovi tugged at his sleeve, steering him away from the confrontation before words could ignite something worse.

The fights kept coming. An archer loosed arrows that split into swarms of light midair. A girl in silver spun her spear in a dazzling blur, each strike leaving arcs of lightning in their wake. Two apprentices fought barehanded, fists wrapped in Bands that struck with the sound of cracking stone.

The arena pulsed with energy, so heavy it made Jax's skin prickle and Tovi's pen stall.

"Everywhere," Tovi whispered. "Everywhere I look, every duel—numbers on display. Proof of rank, proof of worth. And us..." He glanced at his empty wrist, jaw tight. "...nothing."

Jax ignored the sting in the words. His eyes gleamed, drinking in every clash. "Doesn't matter. That's gonna be us. Right there, one day. The noise, the lights, the names...they're chanting names, Tov. Names! You hear it? That's history being written right in front of us."

A roar went up, louder than any before. The next fighter had stepped into the sand. Not one, but three at once, a trio duel. The apprentices moved in perfect triangle formation, covering each other's flanks, weaving strikes that shifted from sword to spell to shield without pause.

The coordination was breathtaking. The crowd thundered their approval, the stone vibrating beneath the boys' feet.

Jax gripped the rail until his knuckles whitened. His grin slipped, replaced by something rawer. A longing, a hunger.

Tovi saw it for what it was and didn't say a word. He only watched, pen silent, eyes behind cracked glass narrowing at the way Jax leaned toward the fight as if his whole body were being pulled forward.

Chapter 13
Duel of Serbalo

The Serbalo Arena quieted in a way that made the air itself feel heavy. Even the vendors at the upper tiers stilled, pitchers paused mid-pour. A horn blared once, sharp enough to make the hairs on Jax's arms rise.

The announcer's voice rolled across the amphitheater, carried by the wards etched deep into the stone:

"Next duel...Rold Varrick of the Harringer Cliffs ... versus Mina Duschene!"

The response was immediate; a roaring wave, thousands of voices crashing together as they bellowed one name:

"ROLD! ROLD! ROLD!"

The boy emerged first. Shoulders broad, axe gleaming with etched runes, he raised it high with practiced flourish. The crowd nearly toppled the stands in their frenzy. His smile flashed like sunlight on steel. He was their champion, the golden heir of the Cliffs, the one everyone expected to carve his place in history today.

The second gate creaked open.

From it strode a girl tightening her training wraps, a stitched half-sun crest flashed under the leather. It wasn't the cracked sun of Yelmers Doom, but its clean, unbroken twin, faded like long forgotten history.

In a box seat, a noble's hand froze; his hands stalling in mid motion to his glass, unsure if what he saw was real.

Mina Duschene didn't raise her hands or flash a smile.

She didn't bow.

Stepping onto the sands she straightened like it was hers already. Her fiery red dreadlocks spilled over her shoulders, her dark skin catching the sun tinting it into a bronzed-gold. The pain leathers hugged her frame. Blades rested across at her back, her gauntlets worn from extensive use tethered at her wrists. There was nothing showy in her gear, nothing noble in her dress.

But her steady, unflinching walk, spoke louder than any cheer.

The crowd didn't acknowledge her. There were comments, some jeers, and a few laughs at the "no-name." Even her surname slipped past most ears. Nobility from elsewhere meant nothing in Icrison. To them, she was just another face to fall before Rold Varrick.

Jax leaned so far forward that his knuckles turned white on the rail. "She's different," he whispered, grin flickering like a lit fuse.

Tovi studied her stance, how she carried her weight, how her eyes never once left Rold. His pen stilled mid-note. "She's not rattled," he said, confused. "Not even a little."

Rold raised his axe high, basking in the thunderous welcome. Mina merely slid one blade free with the soft hiss of metal being released from its binds, and pointed it towards him.

The silence hung thick as the referee lifted his hand to begin, and then it dropped.

Rold exploded forward, axe sweeping in a wide arc that threw sparks as it kissed the stone floor. The crowd roared his name, a chant turned war-drum, pounding with every footfall. Mina didn't flinch. She shifted one step, blade rising to meet him. The clash rang out sharp as struck bells, steel grinding against steel. The force of it shoved her back two paces, boots gouging the sand.

"First hit's his!" someone screamed, the crowd erupting.

Rold pressed, axe carving great crescents through the air, each swing powerful enough to make Jax's chest thud from the impact alone. Mina blocked, turned, slipped aside, her movements small, efficient, unhurried. Each time she gave ground, and each time the crowd grew louder.

"She's getting pushed back," Tovi exclaimed, scribbling in his notebook, glasses flashing against the noonday sun. "But look at her stance, she's conserving, waiting..."

"Waiting?!" Jax bellowed over the chants, voice hoarse. "She's about to get crushed if she doesn't swing back!"

Rold's axe hammered down again, slamming her blade into the ground, spraying sand. Mina bent with the strike, knees almost buckling, before rolling away at the last second. She came up with a streak of dirt across her cheek, eyes still locked steady on her opponent.

The crowd jeered. "Finish her, Rold!" "Don't let her breathe!"

Rold roared and followed, his axe catching the sun in a blaze of runes. The chants beat like thunder. Mina's boots scraped, sliding further as she absorbed the blow, then another.

To Jax, it looked like she was barely hanging on. To many, it looked like she was already beaten.

But her eyes never wavered.

The chants thundered so hard the stone shook.

"ROLD! ROLD! ROLD!"

Emboldened by the crowd's enthusiasm, Rold pressed his advantage; each swing leaving scars in the ground. Mina blocked high, twisted low, slid aside; always a fraction late, always conceding ground. Her blades rang, sparking bright under the sun. The crowd jeered at her backpedaling, their golden boy driving her wherever he wanted.

"She's done for," someone near Jax yelled.

"Not yet!" Jax screamed back, voice cracking. He leaned over the rail, "Fight back!"

On the sand, Mina exhaled once, calm, and slid her second blade free.

The sound was small against the crowd, a clean hiss of steel leaving leather. She rolled her wrists, blades crossing before her in a steady guard. No flourish. Just readiness.

The arena erupted in laughter and scorn.

"She thinks two toys will stop an axe?""Desperation move!"

Rold grinned wolfishly, raising his weapon high. He lunged, his rune-etched edge crashing down with bone-rattling force. Mina's crossed blades caught it, but the impact slammed her boots deeper. She staggered back, teeth clenched, arms trembling.

The crowd exploded at the sight, chanting his name harder.

"ROLD! ROLD! ROLD!"

Jax slammed the rail. "C'mon! You can do this!"

Tracking every shift, every twitch of her stance, Tovi's eyes darted back and forth. A piece of this puzzle didn't make sense to him. Then he saw it; he finally caught what he was searching for. Her eyes glimmered. A faint trail shimmering where they cut across Rold's shoulders, his grip, his footwork. Not magic meant to strike, but to learn; notes written in light.

It happened again when she pivoted around his next blow, her blades scraping the axe's haft before she slipped aside. The faintest flicker in her Band, almost invisible unless you were looking for it.

Tovi's pen stilled, pulse quickening. She wasn't weakening; she was watching, cataloguing him with every strike.

But to the crowd, to Jax, it looked like failure. She hit the dirt once, rolled, and came up slower than before. Dust streaked her dreads, her lip split red. Drawing deeper breaths, her blades shook as she steadied them in front of her.

Rold howled for the crowd, raising his axe high, and they answered him in kind.

Mina expectorated, waving him towards her.

Enraged, Rold barreled forward in response. The runes on his axe flared, its head writhing in firelight as he swung in great, crushing arcs. Each blow split the air with a roar, forcing Mina back; her blades crossing to parry and deflect. The dirt spat sparks where the axe struck, the crowd screaming his name with every near hit.

For a while, Mina gave ground. Her guard was tight as she was drove to the brink of defeat. His confidence swelled with each attack.

Then she stopped. Raising to her full height, Mina allowed her hair to fall over her shoulders, head held high. Her red dreads swung across her face as her eyes locked on his. A slight pause, broke the constant chanting, the breath drawn before a gale.

Her next step was nothing like the last dozen. She slid forward, low and sharp, and Rold's axe whistled through empty air. Her blade struck his exposed flank with a metallic crack, and hush rolling over the crowd as he staggered.

Wind followed her strike. Dust and grit spiraled up, tugging at his cloak, fanning the torch-flames toward him. The axe flared hotter in response, but his swing went wide, bent by a gust that hadn't been there before.

He growled, lunging again. His rune-axe swept in a fiery arc meant to cleave her through, but she wasn't there. She moved past him like a rush of air through reeds, twin blades whistling in a rhythm that felt more storm than steel.

Another blow connected, a shallow test strike, and Rold's boots slid. There was no roar of excitement, just a tense quiet.

Jax slammed both fists against the railing, practically bouncing out of his seat. "That's it! That's how you do it!"

Tovi leaned forward, eyes narrowing. It wasn't brute force that turned the tide. She was reading him, shoulders, grip, breath, and using the smallest tells to slip past. And the gusts that bent his strikes? No rune, no glyphs. Just her.

Steel clashed again, sparks spinning off the blades. Mina pressed harder, blades darting faster. Each whistle of air shoved Rold back another step, his confidence bleeding out with every retreat.

The match had shifted with that single breeze.

Rold's axe came down in another heavy arc, the kind that made the crowd chant his name with every swing. But this time, Mina didn't brace. She slipped. Not backward or sideways; she moved like the strike had been waiting for her, feet gliding across the stone as if the air itself pushed her into place.

The axe hit nothing but dust. The crack of metal on stone rang hollow. For the first time, Rold blinked, caught off-balance.

Mina was already there. A flash of red dreads, twin blades sparking in the light, her body weaving faster than the eye should follow. She cut across his guard, steel ringing against the haft of his axe, forcing him to twist hard just to deflect. The crowd gasped at the sound.

Then came the second strike. And the third. Her blades no longer tested; they commanded. Each one flowed into the next, pushing Rold back step by step. He grunted with the effort, teeth bared, heels scraping furrows across the sand.

Jax leaned forward in his seat, eyes wide. "She's,she's not just faster. She's reading him. Every swing before, she let him think he had her!"

Tovi didn't answer. He was too busy watching the shimmer. The flicker of air curling at her feet, like her movements stirred currents only she could command. Every lunge seemed to carry her further than it should, every dodge tighter than physics allowed. Wind was carrying her, aiding her blades, her steps, and her momentum.

The audience fell into a calm, tension-thickening. No chants, no jeers. Just the ring of steel, the scrape of boots, the realization that the underdog wasn't just surviving anymore. She was hunting.

Mina's lips curled into a grin as her blades blurred again. The match wasn't his anymore.

It was hers.

Rold snarled, shaking sweat from his brow as he reset his grip on the axe. The crowd found its voice again, chanting his name like a shield. The underdog couldn't keep this up forever. She was smaller, untested, reckless. He only had to land one good hit.

He roared and charged, axe cleaving down with all the might a mountain behind it.

Mina didn't flinch. She dropped low, twin blades crossing in an X, catching the strike. The clash cracked like thunder through the arena. Dust flew, sparks leapt. Her knees buckled, arms straining, and then, something rippled.

A cool sheen swept across her blades, translucent and alive. It wasn't metal alone holding that axe at bay anymore. The edge gleamed with liquid shimmer, droplets sliding along the steel as though water itself had been poured into the strike.

The roar of the crowd faltered.

Rold's eyes widened. His axe trembled against her defense, not breaking through, but slowing, caught as though trapped in a current. Mina twisted, and the water along her blades surged like a wave, redirecting the force. His weapon slammed down, kicking up sand instead of bone.

She rose with it. One blade arced high, spraying beads of water that trailed behind like rain frozen in sunlight. The other swept low, fluid and merciless, driving him stumbling backward. He tried to reset his stance, but her strikes poured over him, relentless, un-yielding, like a tide hammering a cliff.

"Did you see that?" Jax shouted, half on his feet. "She, she changed it! She's not just fast anymore, she's..."

"Water," Tovi whispered, in shock. His eyes fixed on the gleam clinging to her blades. Each stroke was heavier, dragging Rold's defenses wider, tiring his arms. The rhythm of her fight had deepened. She wasn't simply outpacing him, she was drowning him.

Rold bellowed, swinging wide in desperation. Mina flowed around it, her twin blades slicing arcs that left faint ribbons of spray in the air. She moved like a storm-tide in human shape, every step heavier, every strike carrying the weight of something vast.

The chants fractured. Some still shouted for Rold, others faltered into silence, and a new sound began to creep in; the hiss of whispers, sharp with awe.

Mina didn't look at the crowd. She only pressed forward, blades hammering, water flashing. The underdog wasn't just holding her ground anymore. She was pulling him into her own tide.

The clash slowed. Rold staggered, axe dragging furrows in the sand as he tried to catch his breath. Across from him, Mina rolled her shoulders, both blades dripping faint trails that hissed as they struck the dirt.

The announcer's voice cut through, loud and straining to mask his own disbelief. "Ro ld of the Harringer Line—pushed back! And the challenger... Mina Duschene, unknown, unranked..."

His words faltered as the hush spread. The audience had no script for this. They had filled the stands to watch their favorite crush an upstart, not to see him stumble under the weight of rain and steel.

A few voices tried to chant Rold's name again, stubborn, desperate. Others hissed them down. A ripple of unease swept the crowd, like a current shifting direction beneath the surface.

Mina didn't bow, didn't preen, didn't even look at them. She spat once into the dirt, blades resting at her sides, and fixed her gaze back on Rold.

It was the announcer who filled the void:"She...she's forcing the veteran back, ladies and gentlemen! Can he recover, or are we seeing the rise of a new name in Serbalo Arena?"

The crowd surged at that, no longer unified. Half roared for Rold to rally, half began a hesitant, broken chant of the girl's name."Mina! ...Mina! ...Mina!"

Her head tilted, as if hearing it for the first time. Her jaw set.

Then she raised her blades again. The liquid that had been trailing from the blades ignited, flames now licking the sands beneath them.

Onlookers were stunned. To the right, Rold's axe burned with the fire of his clan runes, flames streaming from its edge like a banner. And across from him stood Mina, blades ablaze. No runes, no family crest...just her own flames kindling alive.

Cheers of both names erupted from nowhere. Fists pounded against the railing, voices shaking the stones. But a scattering of gasps, whispers, and shrieks curled beneath the chant; the sound of people seeing something they shouldn't be seeing.

Mina moved first.

Her left blade caught Rold's overhead chop. Sparks skittered, sending steel shards shrieking, steel ringing against steel. Her right blade swept in a horizontal arc, fire lashing out like a whip. Rold snarled and swung through it, his runes flaring hotter, a wave of flame forcing her back.

The sand hissed; the nearest wooden pillar blackened from the heat.

Another exchange. His axe came high again, descending like a hammer, fire spilling from the runes. Mina crossed both blades, caught them, then twisted, letting the flames roll off and vanish like smoke on the wind. She spun out of range, blades flashing, and lashed back with her own flames.

The crowd roared with every strike. Jax leaned forward, fists pumping, voice raw from shouting.

Tovi only stared. He couldn't keep up with the speed of their strikes, but he saw the difference. Rold's fire was heavy, a battering ram. Mina's fire was lean, precise. Every swing of her blades were a blaze of razor thin cauterization. Not wild and wasteful.

Her footwork was the same. When she slipped under a downward arc, her heel slid over the sand like she'd mapped each grain's path before stepping. Every parry, every strike was a calculation finished before the swing began.

Through Rold's sweat streaked face, his breath grew ragged. His rune-axe flames began to burn irregular. One second it was bold the next a dullness was seen in his flames.

The crowd's chanting began to slow. The "ROLD! ROLD!" broke, stuttered, then mixed with shouts of another name, uncertain at first, then louder:

"MINA! MINA!"

Rold reeled from a twin-blade slash, his guard faltering. He stumbled, then roared, driving himself forward in a last desperate surge. Fire ripped from his axe, a blazing arc meant to end her.

Mina's blades flared brighter. She brought them down parrying him before launching him back with a kick to the gut. He stumbled a few steps before recovering. Ashamed and frantic Rold tried to launch her skyward, his axe spraying sand as it arced from below. Minas blades caught the axe, fire howling against fire. The arena drowned in heat and light, until Rold's knees buckled. His axe sagged, flames puttering as he hit the dirt.

The crowd erupted, but Mina didn't lower her blades.

She leveled one at his chest, eyes narrowed, stance braced. She thought it wasn't over. She thought he was still coming.

And for a moment, it looked like he was. Rold stirred, groaning as he tried to push himself up.

That was when it happened.

Her right blade, fire dimming at its edge, flickered. Not with red. With white. Then blue. A faint crackle of lightning crawling along the steel, so thin no one in the arena seemed to take note. No one...except Tovi.

He blinked hard, heart kicking in excitement. Sparks? Had she really shown control of four elements?!

Mina's breath for another strike, ready to bring her blade down, only for Rold to collapse again, face-first into the sand, unmoving.

The arena exploded into cheers.

Jax was already on his feet, howling her name like he'd known her all his life. Tovi stayed frozen, staring at her blades. At the place where lightning had been.

He swallowed hard, notebook drooping at his side.

Because if what he saw was real... then Mina wasn't just rewriting the fight. She might be rewriting everything.

Then the crown announcer's voice split the noise like a thunderclap:

"VICTORY! MINA DUSCHENE!"

The name cracked across the stadium, echoed by the voice-mages woven into the stones. The crowd erupted, the sound so loud it felt like the walls themselves might give way. The chants that had been Rold's name now had a new target.

"MINA! MINA! MINA!"

Banners waved. Fists pounded the rail. Children climbed onto their parents' shoulders, shrieking her name. The fire scorched sands still glowed, marking the place where her blades had turned his axe aside.

Jax was shouting so hard his throat gave out, but he didn't care. His fists pumped the air, his grin split wide and wild, eyes shining like he'd just seen a living legend walk out of story and into flesh.

"Did you SEE that?!" he bellowed to no one in particular. "She...she just...BOOM! And then...WHOOSH!" He mimed a blade flurry.

And then his voice cracked higher, the words tumbling out before he could stop them:"She fought like Diestal! Exactly like him..fast, smart, fearless. It was like she knew every move before it even happened!"

Some of the crowd near him turned, startled at the comparison. Diestal's name wasn't tossed around lightly. Jax didn't notice. He was still shouting, still grinning, convinced he'd just seen the first spark of another great.

Tovi's cracked lenses caught the flare of the torches, but his eyes weren't on the crowd. They were locked on her. On the faint image burned into his memory: the crackle, the spark. The fact that she indeed had known Rold's every move by the end of the match.

His hand shook as he wrote. Unregistered affinity? He scrawled the words, underlined them twice, then stared at them like they might leap off the page and explain themselves.

Down below, Mina lowered her blades at last. She didn't bow, didn't strut, didn't even smile. She spat into the sands, rolled her shoulders, and turned her back on the body of Rold as the attendants hurried to carry him away. The chant still thundered, still screamed her name, but she walked like it was nothing new. Like she hadn't just torn down one of the arena's rising stars and burned his fire to ash.

The announcer's voice boomed again, strained with disbelief even as it rang formal:

"Remember the name! MINA DUSKVALE, victorious in Serbalo Arena!"

The chant swelled higher.

Jax's voice tore raw as he kept shouting her name with the crowd. "That's it! That's who we need! She's the third hero!"

Tovi closed the notebook slowly, fingers lingering on the ink that hadn't yet dried. His mouth was dry. His mind raced. Mina Duschene wasn't just skilled. She was dangerous, because she had just shown him something the Bands weren't supposed to allow.

And if no one else noticed? That meant it was his alone to understand.

Chapter 14
After the Roar

The chants hadn't died. Even as the crowd spilled out of Serbalo Arena and into the streets of Icrison, Mina's name rolled like thunder. Flags wagged in the hands of apprentices, the glow of Bands lit the avenues like fireflies, and food sellers shouted over the din trying to hawk roasted skewers and sugar fruit to anyone with a voice left to cheer.

Jax shouldered his way through the throng with a grin that hadn't dimmed since the last clang of her blades. "We're meeting her."

Tovi shoved his cracked lenses up his nose and scowled. "We're not meeting her."

"We are." Jax pointed toward the far side of the arena, where guards in bronze-etched armor held the side gates. "She's in there, walking out right now. All we gotta do is find a way through."

Tovi gaped at him. "Through? Past guards? Past trainers? Do you see the crowd of actual fighters swarming back there?"

Jax didn't even hesitate. "Easy. We do what heroes do."

"Which is?"

"Whatever works."

That was how Tovi found himself crouched beside a supply cart full of blunted practice spears, trying not to gag at the smell of sweat and old wood. Jax slipped one free, spinning it in his hand like he'd carried it all his life. "See? Errand runners."

"You don't even know what that means."

"Doesn't matter if I look like I know," Jax said, already hauling the spear across his back.

Before Tovi could object again, Jax was darting toward a half-open iron grate tucked between two guard towers. The stink hit instantly: old oil, damp stone, the sharp bite of cleaning salts. A service tunnel.

"Jax, no..."

"Jax, yes!" he whispered back, squeezing inside. Tovi groaned but followed, pinching his nose with one hand, clutching his satchel with the other. The tunnel walls were slick with condensation, the air hot and sour, but Jax barreled forward anyway, clanking the spear tip on the stones like it was a torch guiding the way.

By the time they crawled out the far end, both boys were streaked in grime. Jax grinned wider, while Tovi cursed under his breath about infection and sanitation protocols.

The last step was the worst: a guard in bronze armor stood at the corridor mouth, arms crossed, the eight on his Band glowing faintly. His eyes narrowed the instant he saw them. "And what," he growled, "do you mudrats think they're doing back here?"

Jax slapped the practice spear against his shoulder like it was the most natural thing in the world. "Errand runners. Returning practice gear. Important Guild business."

The guard's brow furrowed. His hand slid toward the hilt of his sword.

Tovi's throat dried. This was it. This was how they got thrown in a cell before they even saw the Trials.

But Jax was already digging in his pouch. With a flourish, he pulled out a strip of Rampiro jerky, the kind smoked hard and chewy enough to last a whole hunt. He winked and flipped it at the guard. "For your trouble."

The guard caught it midair, sniffed once, then tore off a bite. His shoulders eased. He jerked his chin toward the inner hall. "Make it quick. And if I see you again, you're both on stable duty."

Jax saluted with the spear and strode past like he owned the corridor.

Tovi staggered after him whispering, "You're going to get us killed before we even…"

"Meet her?" Jax finished with a grin. "Worth it."

The noise of the arena dimmed behind them. Ahead, the torchlit halls of the fighters' quarters stretched into shadow.

The fighters' corridor greeted them with scents of steel and chalk dust. Sweat clung to the stone like smoke after a forge fire. Apprentices limped in from their bouts, trainers barked orders, and attendants carried buckets of water that sloshed dark streaks across the flagstones.

And then she appeared.

Mina.

Her dusty red dreadlocks were tied back, damp from the fight, strands catching the torchlight like copper wire. Her twin blades hung loose at her sides, handled so casually they might've been wooden toys instead of steel that had just brought down Rold. She didn't strut. She didn't bow to the clamor still echoing outside. She walked like none of it mattered, like the victory was already behind her.

Jax's chest tightened. He almost forgot to breathe. Then the words burst out.

"You fight like Diestal!" he shouted, too loud, voice cracking. "Exactly like him! I've never seen anything like…"

Mina's head turned. Her eyes sweeping over him, then Tovi, then their wrists. Dull. Level zero.

Her expression chilled.

"Of course. Zeros."

Jax blinked, caught mid-grin.

"Wait, no, I didn't mean…"

"You didn't mean what?" Her voice was low but edged, words clipped like the strike of her blades. "Didn't mean to hunt me down after my fight? Didn't mean to angle for a free ride on my name? I've seen your kind before." She tapped the air like she was brushing them aside. "Always the same."

Jax stumbled over his words.

"We're not…we don't want a free ride. I mean…well, yeah, we want to fight too, but…"

"You need me?" Her laugh was clipped. "You need to grow up."

Tovi shifted, the satchel tight against his chest. He'd seen that look before: not arrogance, but someone who'd been used and wasn't about to let it happen again. He said nothing, but his gaze lingered. When Mina spat the word "myself," a faint shimmer crossed her Band, like a spark that died before it lit.

No one else seemed to notice.

Jax pressed forward, stubborn fire sparking in his eyes. "You're wrong. You don't know us. You are the third. You're the one we're supposed to fight with. I know it."

Mina's jaw tightened. She turned on her heel, locks snapping with the motion.

"You don't know anything."

She walked down the corridor without looking back, her blades catching the torchlight one last time before she disappeared into shadow.

Jax stood frozen, fists clenched, face red with a mix of anger and awe.

Tovi finally muttered, "Brilliant. First thing she thinks of us? Parasites."

But Jax didn't move. His voice came out rough, low, but burning with certainty. "She'll come around."

The corridors outside Serbalo Arena still rumbled with the echo of chants. The crowd's roar seeped through stone like thunder in the bones. Jax didn't seem to hear any of it. His eyes burned brighter than the torches on the wall.

Tovi trudged beside him, scowling at every step. "She told us no. Clear as daylight. And in case you missed it, she hates us."

Jax waved him off. "She doesn't hate us."

"She called us zeros."

"Okay, she hates us a little," Jax admitted, lips twitching into a grin. "But that doesn't matter." He stopped and Tovi slowed beside him. Jax spun, eyes blazing, voice sharp enough to cut through the hall's clamor. "Because she's the third."

Tovi threw his hands up.

"There you go again...'the third, the third.' Third what? You don't just...decide people are in your story. Heroes don't pick their parties," Tovi pressed, his voice rising. "The world doesn't work like that."

"Yes, it does," Jax shot back. He jabbed a finger at his own chest. "I'm Sangabi...all fire and fearless, charging headfirst no matter the odds." He swung his arm at Tovi. "You're Loria...the Scholar who wrote everything down, always thinking two steps ahead, always knowing what no one else saw." His grin widened, reckless, wild. "And she..." he jerked his thumb over his shoulder, toward where Mina had vanished— "she's Diestal, the blade who carved through armies without blinking."

Tovi froze. His throat went dry.

Loria.

Someone had just said it out loud, about him.

Not mocking. Not scornful. Not the way the others in Wihflan laughed at his books, his notes, his endless scribbles. Jax had looked him in the eye and said it like it was fact. Like it had always been true.

"That's it," Jax said, satisfied, as if he'd solved the puzzle of the universe. "That's us. Sangabi. Lorian. Kael. Our party."

Tovi stammered, trying to find the protest, the logic that would crack the claim apart. "That's...not...you can't..." His voice trailed off, thin and uncertain. His mind screamed it wasn't how the world worked. His chest whispered it was the first time anyone had seen him for what he wanted to be.

Jax clapped him on the shoulder, grinning like he'd already won the argument. "Don't worry, Scholar. You'll get used to it."

Tovi's lips parted, but no words came. His hands falling to his side, the impression of his mothers wand bulging slightly from its side. He shook his head, muttering weakly, "You're insane."

Jax just laughed, loud and unbothered, and strode down the hall like destiny itself had already shaken his hand.

Tovi lingered half a step behind, notebook heavy in his grip, heart hammering with something he didn't want to name.

Chapter 15
Mina

The cheers had faded, but Mina still heard them. They clung to her skin like the dust from teh sands, reverberating in her chest long after she'd left the arena floor.

She kept her stride steady, blades sheathed across her back, head high. Never show the tremor in your hands. Never let them see you flinch. That was lesson one.

The crowd had roared for Rold. His name painted across banners, whispered in taverns, written on betting slips. Rold, heir to the Harringer line, fire's chosen prodigy. And yet, Rold now lay unconscious on the sand, sprawled in the shadow of her victory.

Her victory.

It should've felt like something. Instead it felt like nothing. Just another duel. Just another set of eyes looking at her the way they always did...calculating, wondering how they could use her.

That was lesson two.

She ducked into the quieter passage beneath the Serbalo stands, away from the chanting, away from the smoke and heat. Her boots clicked against stone worn smooth by decades of fighters. She knew this walk. Too well.

The memory rose unbidden: firelight against marble, her father's laugh echoing in the high halls of their estate. Then the shadows. The shouting. The blood.

She shoved it down. Again. Always again.

Lesson three: Don't remember. Don't trust. Don't stay.

They thought she was just another fighter from nowhere, a girl with strange red dreads and a sharper tongue than sense. That was good. That was safe. No one here knew she had once been nobility. No one here knew her family had been betrayed, cut down by the very allies sworn to protect them. No one knew she was the last Duschene.

And it would stay that way.

Mina reached the end of the hall and pressed her palm to the cold stone, leaning into it until her breath evened. Her blades shifted on her back, weight familiar, grounding. She didn't need anyone. Not a guild. Not a partner. Especially not some wide-eyed farm boy and his quiet shadow trailing her with notebooks.

But when she closed her eyes, she saw one thing she hadn't expected in Jax's face. Not hunger. Not calculation. A wild, reckless certainty. The kind she'd seen before, right before the knives turned against her family.

And yet...something in it had been different.

She shoved off the wall, jaw set, and stalked deeper into the guild halls. She didn't need him. She didn't need any of them.

The blade alone...

And that...that was lesson four.

www.ingramcontent.com/pod-product-compliance
Lightning Source LLC
Chambersburg PA
CBHW060339310726
48976CB00007B/2615